A DEADLY REPUTATION

"Must be thirty of 'em," Milt whispered. "I had no idea there'd be that many."

Buck, studying those shadowy men on across the little grassy meadow, said nothing for a long while. He hunkered there with his back to smooth granite, considering this midnight spectacle of wicked-horned Mexican cattle and the half-wild, completely merciless men who had brought them over the line. Eventually he said: "Comancheros, Milt. They're a special breed of men. You never ran across 'em on the north plains. They're the deadliest renegades on earth. They used to trade with the Comanche Indians, but since the Comanches have been reservationed, they've turned to rustling, murdering, robbing…anything lawless and profitable. They never go anywhere except in large gangs."

Milt eased down beside Buckley. "I've heard tales of Comancheros," he said, staring across the meadow. "We got to be damned careful."

NIGHT OF THE COMANCHEROS

LAURAN PAINE

LEISURE BOOKS NEW YORK CITY

A LEISURE BOOK®

October 2005

Published by special arrangement with Golden West Literary Agency.

Dorchester Publishing Co., Inc.
200 Madison Avenue
New York, NY 10016

ISBN 0-8439-5572-4

The name "Leisure Books" and the stylized "L" with design are trademarks of Dorchester Publishing Co., Inc.

Printed in the United States of America.

Visit us on the web at www.dorchesterpub.com.

NIGHT OF THE
COMANCHEROS

TABLE OF CONTENTS

PAID IN BLOOD..1

NIGHT OF THE COMANCHEROS..............47

PAID IN BLOOD

TABLE OF CONTENTS

PAID IN BLOOD......................................1

NIGHT OF THE COMANCHEROS..............47

PAID IN BLOO

ONE

He passed the wrinkled, frayed little slip of dark brown paper to the older man. Both frowned over the unintelligible words scrawled laboriously on it.

K'ad nehee-honisin—dishaah.
J.S.

The older man swore mildly and regarded the message with puzzled wonder. "Makes sense like a poke in the eye with a sharp stick." He turned to Caleb Doorn, regarded Doorn's tense features and fringed hunting shirt, fastened to his narrow waist by a cartridge belt that held a Dragoon pistol and Kiowa-Apache scalping knife with wonder. "Ain't no doubt it's from José Saluc, as the Mex'cans call Tall Horse, but what in hell does it mean? Never heard tell of an Apache who could write before, 'less it's a Mission Injun, an' then they use Spanish, which I don't know, either. But I *do* know this ain't Spanish."

Doorn regarded the little paper thoughtfully. "Come

3

on, Sam'l, let's take it over to Jackson. He'll know what in hell it is."

Samuel Brant made a wry face as he got up and eased his weight gingerly on his game leg. " 'Druther ask a rattler." He fell in beside Doorn's broad-shouldered figure and walked stolidly toward the agency hut of the government civilian in charge of the reservation. Impassive faces went by them in a beady-eyed stream. Uneasy soldiers in bleached and sweat-stained uniforms watched them gravely. The Indians were strange enough, but the half-civilized scouts who wore the dress of Indians and whites alike, with equal aplomb, were beyond their understanding at all. Samuel could see Agent Jackson seated behind his large desk, piled high with crisp papers, through the open door.

"By damn, Caleb, I tell ya this fer the truth. That damned fool in there is goin' to promote a war 'stead of prevent one. Why, the lily-skinned. . . ."

"Forget it, Sam'l. It's not our worry."

"No? Well, b'Gawd, any time my hair's in danger o' leavin' my skull, I sort o' figger it's gettin' awful damned close to bein' a personal affair."

Alger Jackson looked up inquiringly as the two scouts came in on moccasined feet. He tried to force a smile, but there was a rankling animosity in the back of his head for those two men who had deliberately warned him not to take the course he was taking with the Apaches. The weight of his duties and the strain of uneasy responsibility showed plainly on his sweat-streaked face. He said nothing, waiting for the visitors to speak.

Doorn flipped him the little paper. "What's that thing say?"

Jackson studied the note for a long minute, then looked up with cold angry eyes. "Did either of you see José Saluc at the agency today?"

Caleb thought over his answer. He had seen the renegade and recognized him not two hours before. However, he knew, too, that Agent Jackson had sent out strict orders for Saluc to be arrested if he ever returned to the reservation. He finally shrugged noncommittally. "Does it say I did?"

Jackson leaned back in his chair. A rasping squeak grated in the hot atmosphere. "No, not exactly. It simply says that . . . 'You know us . . . we are leaving.' " His face assumed a sardonic expression as he regarded the two men in buckskin. He didn't like them at all, but he was careful. Doorn's reputation had well established him as a venomous and a deadly fearless fighting man. "I naturally assume, since you recognized someone and they were leaving, and their initials are J.S., for José Saluc, that you saw the blackguard on the post." He tossed the scrap of paper on the littered desk. "The thing's written in Navajo, not Apache . . . which fits in nicely, since Saluc was captured by Manuelito's band while a child, was educated in a mission, and is probably the only Apache in the territory who can write English, Spanish, or anything else." He rocked back toward his desk, fixing Caleb with a frosty glance. "Did you see him here today?"

Doorn read the menace in the words correctly. A truthful answer would give Jackson the opportunity he wanted. He could order Doorn's arrest for failure to

5

comply with orders. He let his shoulders rise and fall gracefully. "*¿Quién sabe, jefe? ¿Quién sabe?*"

Jackson's face turned suddenly livid. "Listen to me, Doorn. By Gawd, you'll obey my orders here! I have full authority for dealing with white renegades. They are to be shot out of hand, while the Indians are to get full legal protection. Washington knows what the renegade white men have done out here. They knew it well enough to empower me. . . ."

"Rope it, Jackson!" Caleb's deep-set gray eyes were swimming pools of anger. The agent stopped in mid-sentence and Doorn leaned over the desk to face him. "Your orders were written by men in Washington who left you a lot of leeway because they knew they didn't know what you'd find out here. Now you're interpreting them like a damned fool. You want to force these people to come in and accept government beef. Then you fail to provide the beef, an', when they go out again, disgusted and hungry, you order them arrested like criminals." He flung back off the desk and stood as straight as an arrow, looking down on Jackson. "When are you going to understand that you can't coerce Apaches? When is it going to soak through your thick skull that all they need to go back to warfare is one damned fool stunt by a green agent?"

Jackson came up out of his chair with a wild look in his eyes. "You lie! These savages won't dare go against the soldiers stationed here. They've seen the white man's might."

"Yeah," Samuel Brant interrupted dryly. "An' havin' spent their whole damned lives fightin' against odds no white man in his right mind would tackle, they'll go

6

out in spite of Major Halleck's troops an' Gen'l Grant's hull damned Army, too. Jackson, you're too bullheaded to learn anythin', an' it's a waste of time tellin' ya things we know fer sure. So go to hell your own merry way. All I gotta say is that I hope I'm aroun' when your hair's danglin' from some broncho buck's war bridle." He turned with majestic contempt and stalked out of the office. Caleb traded glares for a second longer, then followed his partner outside where the hot sun struck them like a lowering weight.

When Caleb and Brant were back by Officer's Row, seated in the miserly little dab of shade they found near a log bench, they sat in a musing silence. Alger Jackson just wasn't the man to handle the delicate problem of getting the Apaches to accept the government's bounty. If he couldn't intimidate, then he'd employ force. Brant grunted dourly: "Well, Jackson's goin' to start his own private war afore long. Nothin' we can do about it, an', 'sides, I allow a man'll do well to keep his hair 'thout gettin' too involved, don't you?"

Caleb nodded somberly. "I reckon, Sam'l, only I hate to see trouble come when it's avoidable."

"'Tain't avoidable, Caleb, not when ya got a feather-legged damn' fool like Jackson stirrin' it up. Ain't no way under the sun to head it off." He turned and looked appraisingly at Doorn. "Say . . . when you seen Saluc, how come you didn't say nothin'?"

Caleb shrugged. "He was tradin' melted-down silver jewelry that he probably got from some raid into Mexico. He was dressed like a Navajo, but I know his face too well. We traded stares for few minutes, but I decided against puttin' the soldiers on him because the

7

Apaches on the agency are so restless that any shootin'
at all would start a war."

"So ya let him walk out?"

"Yeah. He hadn't been gone ten minutes when an
old squaw brought me that note."

Brant grunted and regarded his stained old moc-
casins calmly. "Well, he's grateful that you didn't turn
him in or else he wouldn't have sent you that word.
You made a friend, Caleb."

Doorn was watching a group of grave-faced
Apaches approaching Jackson's office. He nodded toward them. "There goes another council to complain
about the delay in the beef ration." They sat lazily and
watched Jackson come out onto his tiny porch and
speak with the Indians through his official interpreter,
a half-breed named Charley Soleil. The Indians were
angry; they were demanding immediate rations. Jackson fought to control himself while the unhappy interpreter sweated and softened the words of both
speakers. Finally one old buck slashed the air with his
arm in the motion of a man cutting a picket line. Jackson glared at him solemnly for a long moment, then
his answer came clear and brief across the stilled compound to watching Indians and soldiers alike.

"If any more of you leave the agency, I will send the
soldiers to hunt you down like coyotes." For a long,
awful moment there wasn't a sound, then the Apaches
murmured among themselves, turned abruptly away
from Jackson, and stalked off. Caleb shrugged and
spoke without looking at Brant.

"There it is, Sam'l, that's all the Apaches needed . . .
one strong threat."

8

Brant filled a stubby pipe, lit it carefully, puffed a big cloud of bluish smoke, and spat emphatically. "Aw right, the damned idjit asked fer it. But I ain't stickin' by a man who ain't got the brains God give a lizard. Hell, gettin' killed's one thing, but bein' slaughtered because of a fool an' his ignorance is another. I'm goin' to ride for Fort Defiance. At least they got an old Army man in command there, not a satchel-packin' civilian." He arose meaningly. "You comin'?"

Caleb shook his head. "No, Sam'l, I'm goin' to try an' keep the soldiers from spillin' all their blood in the trouble that's comin'." He wagged his head slightly. "It ain't their fault, but they'll have to take the brunt of the Apaches' fury. No, you go ahead, explain to Colonel Edmonds over at Defiance what's goin' on, an' see if you can talk him into workin' with Major Halleck's command. Lord knows, Halleck's goin' to need help. I'll stay here an' work with the soldiers."

Brant stood looking down at Caleb in indecision for several minutes. He hated to leave his old partner; still, as Doorn had said, Halleck's command was going to need help. If the troops from Fort Defiance would throw in with the agency patrolmen, at least there wouldn't be any massacre. That, after all, was better than trying to gain a decisive victory in a wild, endless land where Indians came and went like wraiths. He grunted disgustedly and walked off toward his horse.

Doorn watched the older man go in speculative silence. He didn't take his eyes off Brant until a soft shadow fell across his vision, then he turned and looked up into the sweaty and troubled face of a lean, wiry cavalryman whose faded blue eyes were set in a bronzed face that had the set muscles and defiant look of an old campaigner.

"Howdy, Major."

Halleck sat down in Brant's recently vacated place on the log bench. "Caleb, that gawd-damned Jackson's gone an' riled 'em good this time."

"I reckon. We heard it 'way over here."

Halleck's jaw worked rhythmically on a small quid of chewing tobacco. Discontent was stamped deeply into his hawkish features. "The damned fool! At best we got only a finger hold here. By settin' the Indians on their ears, we'll lose everythin' we've fought like hell to accomplish for the past year."

Caleb nodded at the bitterness in the major's voice. "I reckon. Well, it's torn now, Major. There's only one of two things left to do. Either fight 'em to a stand-still . . . which we can't do with the limited troops available . . . or pony up on our promises . . . which won't happen as long as Jackson's in charge here."

Halleck leaned back on the bench and turned a quizzical look on Doorn. "Caleb, do you think the reason the cattle aren't bein' delivered is because Jackson's peddlin' them on the side?"

Caleb had heard this suspicion voiced before. It was a common practice with dishonest Indian agents, but he didn't believe Jackson was the type. He was a fool, a bureaucrat, and a man loaded with conceit and arrogance, but he wasn't a thief. "No, Jim, I don't think Jackson's a renegade. He's just about everything else, but I don't believe he's dishonest."

Halleck nodded thoughtfully. "I don't think so, either, but he's sure a horse's. . . ."

"Major Halleck!" Both men looked up. Agent Jackson was standing near the bench. Halleck nodded without getting up. Apparently Jackson hadn't heard himself blistered by the scout and the officer. "You'll send out patrols to watch the Indians. I have reason to believe they're plotting treachery."

Halleck made a wry face. "I wouldn't be surprised."

"What do you mean, sir?"

Halleck got up. He towered a head taller than the agent. "Why in hell don't you figure your beef-delivery schedules so that the herds are on the reservation before the last delivery is exhausted?"

Halleck's face was granite-hard and accusing. Jackson gave him stare for stare and answered in an icy tone. "You overreach your authority, Major. See that patrols are doubled and activated at once." He turned and walked stiffly away, hesitated, turned back, and motioned to Caleb. "Mister Doorn, come with me." Doorn arose, tossed a dour grin at Halleck, and walked after the Indian agent.

11

TWO

Major Halleck was mustering the troops when a lathered horse thundered across the parade compound, slid to a halt before Jackson's office, and the rider hit the ground, running. Halleck felt a tightening in his entrails as he watched the man burst into the agent's office, but he faced back toward his non-coms and gave the usual orders.

Caleb was leaning against the wall, studying the agent, who was complaining about the lack of cooperation with the agency when the wild-eyed youngster burst in upon them. Both looked up in surprise. The boy wasn't more than sixteen years old with the long hair and buckskin clothing of one of the outlying settlers who were battling nature and Indians alike in a courageous effort to carve a ranch out of the turbulent land.

"Mister Jackson!" Jackson nodded and the pinched face turned away from Caleb. "'Paches 'tacked our ranch. I slipped away an' come here for help."

"How long ago?" Caleb took the words out of Jackson's mouth.

The boy turned toward him imploringly. " 'Bout two hours ago. They're still fightin' us . . . I mean, m'father an' mother an' sister are holdin' 'em off from inside the cabin."

Doorn jerked his head toward Jackson. "Better send Halleck out right away." He started for the door. "I'll tell him." The scout was gone before Jackson could say a word. He turned back to the boy as the sudden blast of a bugle shrilled wildly outside and the dull thunder of running men and shouted orders filtered back to them. "What's your name, lad?"

"Mike Callahan. We've got the land over by Owl Crick."

Jackson nodded. He knew the family. He wrote something on a piece of paper and spoke without looking up. "I'll make a report of the action. You. . . ."

"Report be gawd-damned!" Mike was running back to his horse when Jackson looked up, startled. Anger flooded through him again. He was beginning to hate all Westerners, not just the surly, independent scouts and the grumbling soldiers but the impatient settlers as well. Nowhere, since coming to his new position as Apache agent, had Alger Jackson found any restraint or respect for his position.

He got up slowly and moved to the doorway. A patrol of troopers loped past, followed by others. None looked his way as they cleared the massive old pole gate and struck out across the shimmering land. He saw Jim Halleck and Caleb Doorn riding to one side of the column and suddenly it dawned on him that he hadn't ordered the soldiers out at all. Doorn had passed the word. He watched Caleb's broad back disappear through the stockade with a slow lust for revenge building up inside of him.

The fighting was still in progress, which was unusual. Marauders—whether Apaches, Comanches, or northern tribesmen—usually hit hard and fast and left the same way. Doorn reported back by heliograph. Halleck split the command and waited until the outriding half were far enough around the battered ranch to cut off the raiders. Then the bugler let loose his piercing notes of vengeance and the troopers came over the range like a ragged line of avenging angels, sabers extended, savage yells of exultation rumbling past cracked and bleeding lips that seemed to come out of their bowels, fringed with hate and the lust to kill the murderous enemy.

Doorn, riding on the outer edge of Halleck's section, saw the startled looks flash over the Indians' faces. They were caught completely by surprise. For a long second, even the screams of the cavalrymen died down and only the irregular thunder of the horses' hoof beats rolled in the diminishing distance. The land appeared to be lying still and fearful, waiting for the clash of the ancient enemies. Then the Apaches scurried for their horses. They would fight mounted. The action was belated, however, for the thin blue lines were in among them before less than half could get to a horse. The wild yells were punctuated by an ominous, dull sound as carbines were pressed into bellies and fired. Sabers flashed in murderous arcs and the sun glinted crazily off them. Words ripped out in Spanish, English, and Apache, each saying basically the same thing—kill or be killed!

Caleb held his pistol balanced like a fine instrument, its barrel tilted a little. Suddenly a dismounted hostile, watching from a clump of brush, leaped at Jim Halleck, grabbed the officer's leg, and raised a muscular hand bent into a volatile fist from which shone the stubby blade of a knife. Caleb took calm aim and fired. The brave went over sideways as though huge fingers had flung him away. For a fleeting second Halleck's white face, looking back toward Caleb, shone, then he regained his seat and was gone in the raucous turmoil.

The roar and acrid smoke of battle swirled in a wild pillar, churned by fear-crazed horses. Over near the house, a mounted trooper was spurring after a wildly running hostile. He gained rapidly, and the Apache spun and yanked the inevitable knife from his breechclout—a futile, defiant gesture for the trooper's immense saber swung lazily through the air, feet longer than the knife. The Apache tried to duck the blow. The trooper's wrist turned an inch to compensate for the wily foe's feint and the blade struck the man leeward of his head, bit through the corded muscles of his neck, down through his collar bone, into his lungs, shattering ribs like twigs until its momentum was stopped near the navel. Caleb turned away as the trooper fought to extricate his blade from the quivering flesh.

It was over almost as quickly as it had started. Halleck passed the order for a muster, tallied the casualties, found that he had one dead and four wounded. The Apaches had left seven dead and two unable to mount horses. He sent the wounded, white and red, back to the agency, mopped his glistening forehead, and turned toward Doorn: "Caleb, ride over to the cabin an' see who's left alive, will you?"

Doorn nodded, and reined away.

The raw-boned man watched Caleb ride up. They traded glances. Caleb saw the prototype of all emigrants—flat-stomached, cold-eyed, and thin-lipped, with a built-in propensity for absorbing punishment and an equally obvious ability to give it. He had forgotten the boy who had brought the message of the attack until he saw him beside the big settler. He reined up, and nodded. "Callahan?"

"Yep, that's me, but damned if I'd've taken any bets on what they'd've called me an hour ago."

Doorn nodded.

"We was sittin' down to the noon meal when they rode in on us. Damned lucky we was in the cabin."

Again the mounted man nodded.

"Mike seen 'em first. We barricaded the place an' fought 'em till you fellers got here." He looked at his half-grown son with a wavering grin. "Mike figgered he could slip past 'em, an' I reckon he did."

Caleb caught the words as they rolled off Callahan's lips, but his glance went over the rancher's head to the slim figure of a girl who stood silhouetted in the bullet-scarred cabin doorway behind them. He heard a cavalryman riding up. Major Halleck's voice came into the conversation. Caleb didn't hear what he was saying, but reined past the rancher and rode up to the cabin.

Her taffy hair was long and gently wavy above a thinly sprinkled nest of freckles that set off the violet eyes and rosebud mouth.

"Miss Callahan?"

She nodded.

Caleb watched the pulse in her throat. "Are you all right? You an' your mother?"

She nodded again, her eyes lost in the somber depths of his gaze. She forced herself to speak. "Yes. We're all right, thank God. You are Mister . . . ?"

"Caleb Doorn, a scout from the agency."

That seemed to bring her back. A shaft of fire spiraled from the violet eyes. "Then maybe you can tell us why the Apaches are marauding off the reservation. Alger Jackson himself told us there would be no more raiding."

Caleb nodded regretfully. "Perhaps Jackson was mistaken. At any rate. . . ."

"At any rate, we were attacked by agency Indians."

"How do you know they weren't some of José Saluc's renegades?"

She snorted mildly. "Renegades! José Saluc is no renegade. The renegades are the bucks who have left the agency out of defiance. Saluc left it because he was starving. Does that make him a renegade?"

Caleb fought to control the smile that pushed its way forward. In her indignation she was beautiful, yet there was something irresistibly amusing about her girlish wrath, too. "How could you know they weren't renegades?"

She was calming down. The sudden relief was taking hold of her now, and the tension lessened. "Because we know most of the agency Indians, and there were reservation bucks in the band that attacked the ranch."

"Are you certain you recognized some of the hostiles?"

"Of course."

Doorn turned and waited for Halleck to come up, then he told the officer what the girl had said. Halleck's faded eyes widened at the slim, full-breasted figure in the doorway. He only half heard what Doorn told him. "Is that so?" he said in a soft voice.

Caleb responded: "I reckon it is. At least, the young lady says so."

"Catherine," her father put in.

Caleb and the officer both nodded in appreciation.

"Catherine says so, Major."

Halleck nodded gravely. "Then, Mister Doorn, they were definitely tame ones turned broncho?"

Caleb's laughing eyes were fully on the girl's face when he answered. "Without question, Major."

Jim Halleck inclined slightly from the waist. "Without question, Mister Doorn."

The rancher looked bewilderedly from one man to the other, wagged his head slightly, and walked back toward the bivouacking troopers who were far more interested in drinking from his carefully bricked-up spring than they were in admiring his beautiful daughter.

The troops started back just as the sun nestled into a distant notch in the cordon of distant mountains. They rode back into the agency compound as the last sad notes of retreat sang out in lonely, haunting rhythm over the ravished land. Major Halleck mustered and dismissed his men, took a verbal summons to the agent's office, exchanged significant glances with Doorn, and strode across the iron-like parade area erect and tired to the bone.

Halleck was braced to receive a flood of acid rebuke, but Jackson was visibly shaken and slumped when the officer strode in. He looked up absently, studied the dusty, faded man before him, then spoke in the dull, dry tones of a man who is being whittled at by conditions he can neither control nor understand.

"They're gone, Major."

"Who?"

"The tame Apaches, Major. They've left the agency. There's only a handful left. Somehow I've fumbled my assignment."

The officer sat down squarely on a camp stool. Weariness and lethargic disillusionment leeched the spirit out of him. All the sweat and strain of a year's campaigning to bring the Apaches into line had been wiped out by the man before him—all of it, including the dead troopers buried in forgotten graves. He studied his scarred boot toes without saying a word.

Jackson's gaze went over him callously, as though Major Halleck were a piece of camp equipment. "What have I done wrong, Major?"

Halleck didn't answer right away. He rolled it over in his mind. If Jackson couldn't see any of the failures himself, then he probably wouldn't see them any clearer if he were told of them. He shrugged indifferently and started to get up.

"No, stay right there." There was a tenor to Jackson's voice that Halleck had never heard before. "Tell me, Major, what have I done wrong?"

Halleck regarded his civilian superior gravely. Jackson was a typical desk bureaucrat. He unbuttoned the upper three buttons of his tunic so the cool night air could mingle with the sour sweat that drenched him. "Everything, Jackson, every gawd-damned thing. Doorn told you not to try force, but you told him you were in command here. You fouled up the beef herd delivery schedules some way . . . although any damned fool would know that the Indians would stay on the agency only as long as they were fed. You ordered out patrols to keep 'em on the reservation by force, when the Apaches outnumber the troops three to one, not counting the lads from Fort Defiance. You won't listen to the Indians when they come in for a council. Sure, they're ignorant, unwashed savages, but you let 'em know *you* think they are, too, an' that's a bad mistake to make with Indians." He waved a tired arm in resignation. "Everything you've done so far, Jackson, has been the wrong thing, an' you're too damned butt-headed to see it." He turned and started through the door. "All right, Mister Agent Jackson, you made the damned bed, now, by Gawd, you can lie in it."

The thin finger of orange light didn't die out in Jackson's office until the night was half spent. Hollow-eyed and with mottled spots of stagnant blood showing under his skin, the Indian agent sought his quarters. Sleep evaded him, however, and the alkali of his defeat played havoc inside his skull. He was up and shaved with the cool first rays of dawn. He sent a sentry to fetch Doorn and Major Halleck. Both men showed up at Jackson's office just as the agent opened the door for the day's business. He forced a wan smile and motioned the men inside. "Sit down, gentlemen, sit down."

Major Halleck threw a startled glance at Caleb. They sat.

"Now, then, gentlemen, I've spent the night in thought and have come up with some new ideas."

Caleb groaned to himself.

Halleck's face was still puffy with sleep. "Couldn't they have waited until after breakfast?"

Doorn smothered a smile and Jackson shook his head emphatically.

"No. I'm afraid not. Now, then, Major Halleck, I want you and Caleb Doorn to tell me what to do."

Doorn's eyes were fastened in astonishment on the agent. He blinked owlishly at Halleck. "What do you mean?"

Jackson sat down and smiled hopefully. "Just what I've said. I've messed up the entire program out here. I can see that now, an' I apologize for being obstinate and ignorant. Now, starting today, you two . . . er . . . *hombres* will run the agency unofficially. In other words, you tell me what to do, an' I'll see that it's done. Understand?"

Major Halleck ran a disbelieving hand through the grizzled shock of hair that had recently served him as a pillow. "Well, it's probably too late, now that the Apaches are gone, but we can sure try it, eh, Doorn?"

"I reckon."

Jackson looked relieved. "What's our first move, then?"

Halleck turned to Doorn, who sat with his head cocked, listening to the sounds of a running horse. "Unless I'm plumb mistaken, *hombres*, our first move is comin' in on a run right now."

The three of them walked outside and watched a cowboy descending upon them. He had a dirty white bandage coiled haphazardly around his head. Jackson was biting his lips as the man set his horse up with a fine spray of flying gravel and slid off.

"Who's Agent Jackson?" The man's hard face was drawn with pain and anger.

Halleck jerked his head toward the agent.

The rider walked forward, his spurs making a musical jingle as he came up close. "Your damned 'Paches are runnin' fer the border an' attackin' every ranch 'tween here an' thar."

THREE

Jackson swallowed hastily and felt his eyes falter before the venomous stare. "I'm sorry, but, really, it's not my fault, y'know." He felt two other sets of eyes on him and let the words fade away. "Major Halleck, we'll have to have action."

The cowboy swore obscenely. "Is that all you got to say, you damned white-skinned little horny toad? Why, fer half a gawd-damned cent I'd. . . ."

"Rope it, cowboy!" Caleb's sunken eyes were baleful. "If you're lookin' for someone to blame, why not go after the hostiles?"

The rider's face went bleak and the breath came through his teeth like steam from a pop-off valve. "Step soft, squawman. By Gawd, I've killed better men. . . ."

"Then go for your gun, hardcase!"

Halleck and Jackson barely had time to throw themselves sideways when a snarled oath and two crashing gunshots split the early morning quiet. They heard the excited yells of aroused troopers coming on the run when they got back to their feet and looked around. Caleb was still standing, a thin streamer of dirty white smoke trickling from the black barrel of his pistol. The cowboy was holding a bleeding hand and swearing in a sort of regulated rhythm, staring hard at Doorn in animal fascination.

"You had it comin', cowboy. Now, if you're satisfied, pick up your gun an' get on your horse. We'll get to horse an' be with you in a minute."

Major Halleck and Caleb went down toward the enlisted men's quarters where the officer had the bugler call out the men.

Jackson avoided the bleeding hand of the rider. Blood, even someone else's, always made him sick.

"You got a man, there, Agent, damned if you ain't. What's his name?"

Jackson smiled weakly. "Caleb Doorn. He's. . ."

"By Gawd, I should've knowed it. Caleb Doorn! Well, hell, it ain't no shame to be shot by him."

"No? Well, I've. . ."

"Aw, go suck eggs!" The cowboy turned away from Jackson as though he just remembered seeing the agent. He made a crude bandage out of a filthy handkerchief and walked over to his horse, swung aboard, and reined down toward where the troopers were forming.

"Jim?"

"Yes."

"You'd better go tell Jackson this will probably be the main campaign an' have him get word to Fort Defiance to keep patrols out so's they can keep tabs on us, just in case we stumble onto the whole bunch of tribesmen."

Halleck nodded, accepted his horse from an orderly, swung up, and frowned. "I'd better have him get the wagons loaded and sent out after us under convoy, too. If we trail 'em to the border an' catch 'em, it'll be several days before we get back."

Caleb nodded as the officer swung away. He turned to find the cowboy staring at him. He regarded him coldly.

"Say, Doorn, where'd you fellers get that there agent, anyway?"

"He was sent out to replace old Evans, who died about eight weeks ago."

"Well, by Gawd, you could've got a Injun kid fer an agent an' he'd've done better, I reckon."

Caleb shrugged, watched Jim Halleck ride back, then the column moved out and swung south. Halleck eyed the cowboy with obvious displeasure, turned abruptly and faced Caleb.

"The damned fool gave us full rein after the trouble's started. He's not so dumb. If we fail, he can blame us for everything."

Doorn nodded. "I got that feeling when he told us we were to run the show from now on, back in his office. He's evidently afraid and figures he's in about as bad a mess as he can be in anyway, an', if by some fluke, you an' I can salvage something out of the wreckage, he'll save his job. If we fail, he can say we've taken the power away from him and used it arbitrarily."

Halleck swore. "Nice mess."

"Not too bad, Jim, not if we can catch the bronchos before they get over the border."

"What makes you think we can?"

"This is the trace they used to use, an' so far I haven't seen a single unshod horse track."

"So?"

"So, they're doin' a little raidin' before they head south . . . which means they'll be after horses, guns, and ammunition among other loot before they strike out for Mexico."

"I see. They ought to be pretty well slowed down with loot, then, hadn't they?"

"I reckon. But we've got to hustle all the same. You've got to spread out an' be ready to move damned fast when we get word they're comin' down the land."

Halleck agreed thoughtfully. His spirits came up a little. Maybe it wasn't hopeless, after all. He turned and looked down the long column of twos, plodding along in the deceptive coolness of early morning with the patience and stubborn resolve of the cavalryman, then his glance fell on the cowboy.

"You'd better return to your outfit, *hombre*."

"We're headed thataway. I'll cut off when we hit the elm bottoms near San Saba Pass."

"Anybody killed when they hit you?"

"Naw. Jes' me an' another rider banged up a little, but they sure made off with a nice remuda of California-bred horses."

Halleck grunted and swung back in the leather, his brooding eyes fastened on the invisible distance where destiny was setting the stage for the oncoming actors.

* * *

The sun was a brass knob hung overhead when the blue column swung down along the wasteland they knew marked the dividing line between Mexico proper and the United States. Just exactly where the line ran, no one knew for certain. At one time American surveyors had piled little cairns of rocks every half mile or so, but angry Mexicans had scattered those markers. Consequently neither side knew for sure where the boundary line was. It really didn't matter much, anyway. Whoever showed up with the largest force invariably established the line where he wanted it, and today it was the United States Army under Major Jim Halleck of the Lone Pine Apache Agency who was riding parallel to the border.

The troopers were dismounted at a small brackish puddle that was laconically called Willow Springs. Videttes were sent out fan-wise to seek sign of the oncoming raiders. Major Halleck sweltered and swore. Caleb Doorn sat in the shade of his mount and grinned up at the officer.

"Usin' language unbecoming an officer won't set right with Agent Jackson."

Halleck made a startling observation regarding the probability of Jackson's maternal descent coming from an immediate source of crafty canines and sank down on the hard earth. "When I get back, damned if I don't think I'll ride over to Defiance an' send my resignation in through channels. This here mess has got my goat, damned if it hasn't. Jackson's gone an' maneuvered you an' me into a jackpot for sure. Win or lose, he wins an' we lose . . . plus the fact that he might get killed because of his silly blunders."

Caleb's keen ears caught the sound of a loping horse. He turned and studied the desert with a puzzled frown. If any of Halleck's videttes was coming in so soon, it could only mean that the Apaches had seen them and laid back in wait. The sound became easily distinguishable, then Doorn saw the rider. There was something familiar about the casual way the man sat the saddle. Moreover, he wore buckskin instead of a uniform. "I'll be damned if it isn't Sam'l."

"Where?"

Caleb jutted his chin just as Brant cleared the last fringe of brush and swung in toward the spring. Halleck pushed himself up with a frown. "What in hell's the old fool doin', ridin' around alone, an' how come he's down this way?"

"Howdy, hoss." Sam'l dismounted, winced as his game leg hit the ground, and forced a sweaty grin. "Can't catch no hostiles settin' aroun' a mud puddle."

"How come you to know we were here, Sam'l?" the major asked.

The old scout cocked a speculative eye at Halleck. "Soldiers from Fort Defiance was called out early this mornin' to pertect a rancher. Colonel Edmonds sent me to the agency to find out just what in hell Jackson's done to stir up this here hornet's nest. When I got to the reservation, Jackson tol' me I'd find you lads down here maybe, an' I trailed you. He said you was huntin' hostiles. That right?"

"We're waitin' for 'em, Sam'l. Figure they'll strike for the border as soon as they're full o' loot."

Samuel sat down on his haunches and nodded. "Good figgerin', *hombres*, on'y they're goin' to cross about five miles north o' here."

"How do you know?"

"I cut some sign comin' over this mornin' that makes me cal'clate it like that."

Caleb turned to Halleck. "That's good enough for me, Jim, let's go."

Halleck swore with feeling and ordered the men to horse. The afternoon sun was scorchingly hot. It burned the lungs raw with each indrawn breath. "All right, let's ride, boys. Damn the Apaches an' Jackson an' this burned-out corner of hell, too."

The column had videttes flung out on both sides with Doorn and Samuel Brant ranging like hunting dogs ahead. They hadn't gone more than two miles from Willow Springs when Doorn reined up and swung around in the saddle. He could see the serpentine line of the cavalry behind him, like blue centaurs robed in their own lazy dust, while far off were the outriders, pursuing a parallel course. Aside from the immediate body of men, the great vault of land looked dead and deserted. He turned back and looked over at Samuel Brant.

"Sam'l, if the hostiles head south ahead of us, they'll see us before we see them, unless we keep that fringe of brush up ahead between the two parties."

"I reckon. Beyond that 'ere fringe is the open range . . . not a stick o' cover fer a mile. We'd better hold up until we see 'em. I'll go back an' tell the major."

"Yeah. An' tell him to pull in those videttes. They stick out like a sore thumb."

Brant was turning to ride back when a rifle crashed up ahead. Caleb threw himself sideways, but Brant's horse gave a prodigious lunge and toppled over. Samuel sat stunned for a second, then bounded to his feet with streamers of profanity rushing past his lips. Caleb flung a startled glance at the brush up ahead, saw nothing, whirled, and grabbed Samuel's arm, flinging him up behind the saddle. Three ragged shots followed them.

The echoes drifted slowly down to Halleck. He squinted into the distance, saw Caleb riding downwind like a flying demon with Samuel's hunched-over figure behind him, and shouted an order back to the non-coms. The column came to life, tossing off the lethargy inspired by the blast furnace heat, and swung in behind its commanding officer. Sabers slid raspingly out of metal scabbards and the rolling crescendo of running horses made an ominous sound in the fiery stillness.

Halleck waved as he rode past and Caleb jettisoned Brant. His horse was winded and shaking as much from fear as from exertion. Together, the scouts watched the column swing into ranks of fours and hurtle past. Samuel tested his game leg, found it uninjured, and swore a mighty oath.

"Ain't no big party. Scouts, more'n likely."

"Yeah. It was a party of scouts, but why in hell they fired on us is beyond me . . . unless they're bravo bucks with a skinful of stolen whiskey."

Samuel watched the troopers fan out through the

brush. Suddenly a rattle of musketry floated back, muted and soft. "Them damn fools'll learn not to jump a hull army o' cavalry after this, I allow."

Caleb saw wave after wave of troopers break over the fringe of brush. Suddenly the firing swelled to a crescendo. Cavalrymen began to fall back through the trampled brush. A ragged little group of riderless horses appeared, stirrups flopping, heads high. Samuel was erect and straining to see what had happened. Doorn's voice cut into his thoughts like a dousing of cold water.

"Ambush, b'Gawd! The Apaches was just beyond the fringe in force. They baited the troopers into chasin' their scouts."

"Go rope me one o' them loose horses, Caleb. Gawddammit, we got to get up there."

Caleb mounted in a flying leap, spun away, and headed for the nearest group of bewildered horses. The animals, strangely enough, didn't run from him until he was almost among them. Then they caught his scent. But he got one with small effort and loped back to Brant, who mounted on the fly and tore out behind his partner, unlimbering the carbine that jolted under his leg in the saddle boot. Neck and neck they covered the distance to where all the bedlam of a full-scale war was increasing with each moment. Samuel turned toward Caleb and shouted against the hot wind that flew between them.

"Can't figger why they'd pick a fight this near the line. They coulda' slipped across it an' the soldiers couldn't't've gone after 'em."

Caleb shook his head. "They aren't that dumb, ol'

hoss. They know damned well the soldiers'd follow them twenty miles into Mexico before they'd turn back. Halleck would swear to his dyin' day he thought the line was farther south."

Brant turned this over in his mind. He knew it had happened many times, just as Caleb said. He shrugged and watched as his mount plunged recklessly through the angled brush. Then the racket of the conflict brought him face to face with a wild, surging, pitched battle and he saw to his surprise that the Apaches were fighting in force—which proved that the scouts had deliberately fired on them in order to create an illusion of a small force, thus drawing the main body of troops out onto the plain where the hostiles were eagerly awaiting to fight them toe to toe.

A lance-bearing hostile bore down on Brant with a screech that made the old scout's scalp lock bristle. He threw down with the carbine, firing one-handed. He missed and narrowly escaped being skewered by the pole. As the Indian flashed past, they exchanged taunts in Spanish. Samuel flung the carbine aside, yanked his pistol, and took out after the Apache. His first shot made the savage drop his lance. The second toppled him from his horse, even as Brant felt his own horse fault under him. He barely kicked free of the stirrups before the animal plunged to earth and Samuel, for the second time that day, was catapulted forward like a cannonball. He fetched up hard against a corded pair of legs and found himself staring into a rabid and startled pair of obsidian eyes. He swung desperately with his clubbed pistol, felt the face give way sickeningly under the violent impact, sprang to his feet, and darted toward a group of embattled cavalrymen fighting while dismounted.

Caleb never saw the savage who clubbed him hard between the shoulder blades. It wasn't until he was flat on the ground and saw a man flinging off his pony, knife bared for the *coup de grâce*, that he knew what had happened. Fuzzy but conscious, he rolled away as the Apache leaped. It was a fight for time. If the Apache got to him, he knew he was doomed. He needed a few seconds to get his faculties back into operation. The blow, plus the fall, had partially stunned him. Screaming oaths in three languages, the big buck, a head taller than most of the Apaches—who were seldom over five feet eight inches in height—bore in. Caleb lashed out with his toe. The brave took the blow lightly in the stomach, roared in fury, and made a looping slash with the knife. Caleb was clearheaded now and his own heavy-handled knife was out and darting like the cold steel tongue of a deadly snake.

Caleb got the man's gauge after he had feinted him twice. Every time the big Indian lunged at the scout, he would use his knife in an overhand stroke, as if he were swinging a hatchet. Caleb smiled, and the confidence made the Apache scream his obscenities in a wilder voice as he threw caution to the wind and bore in, his knife coming down high and fast. Caleb slid in low, dropped to one knee, and brought his own knife in and upward. He could feel the tearing of the skin and flesh as the knife hit upward and lodged against the buck's breastbone. Quick as a flash he yanked back and ducked out from under the suddenly erratic knife of the dying man.

A gun exploded close behind. He dropped low and spun away, flashing his hand to his own holster. Two wild-eyed hostiles were coming in. They had been watching the fight, certain their fellow tribesman would kill the white man in buckskin. Now they were bent on vengeance.

Caleb fired twice. One of the Apaches went over backward with his hands thrown up over his face, which had suddenly mushroomed into a welter of scarlet gore, but his second shot missed. The Apache raised his gun when a brilliant stroke of lightning flashed blindingly out of nowhere and hit deeply into the broncho buck's back. He made an awful scream and went over forward, his gun going off heavenward. Caleb got a brief glimpse of Jim Halleck through the shambles and darted back into the thick of the fight.

In a sudden clearing, where the gunsmoke was above his head, Caleb took a quick look around and saw Apache women and oldsters herding the hostiles' horses back out of rifle range. He ran back through the press of deafening gun thunder and found Brant polishing off a brace of drunken braves who had tried to stalk him. He grabbed the scout and plunged on toward where a group of cavalry mounts were tangled in their reins. Selecting two of the freshest-looking horses, they mounted on the fly, reined around, and tore back to where Caleb saw Jim Halleck, legs spread, gun in one hand and slashing saber in the other. He jerked the officer off balance and leaned down to yell in his ear.

"Get the bugler, Jim. Have him blow retreat. Mount your men."

"Retreat like hell! We won't leave this field until. . ."

"Gawd-dammit, Jim, Sam'l an' I are going to stampede their horses. When they see they're afoot, they'll make a break for your horses. Whoever is mounted after I run off the Indians' horses has won."

He didn't wait for an answer. Samuel followed as they skirted the kaleidoscope of roaring action and rode down upon the huddled Indian remuda behind its wall of human guards. The Apaches saw them coming and began a shrieking wail. Several fired guns. Dimly Caleb heard the bugler blow a ragged and hurried call to horse. The Apache women were waving knives, and some had pistols they had picked up from fallen troopers. Brant swung a cavalry saber he had found hanging in the steel scabbard of his mount. They flashed through the wall of bodies and into the panic-stricken herd of horses, Samuel swinging the saber sideways, dealing out indiscriminate and stinging blows and Caleb shouting at the top of his voice and firing over the horses.

In spite of the frenzied efforts of the Apaches to hold back the horses, the maddened animals charged over them and fled in a belly-down run out over the flat range, ears back and nostrils distended. They were running as far and as fast as legs and lungs would carry them, away from the awful smell of fresh blood, and the insane roar of the battle. Dimly Caleb and Brant heard a great wail go up from the Indians. They had seen their horses being stampeded. Caleb held up his arm, and Samuel reined beside him. Together they watched the horses becoming smaller and smaller as they charged to freedom. Then they swung back toward the battlefield. Already the firing was dying down. The Apaches were afoot and facing the mounted cavalrymen. They saw the utter futility of continued resistance. Caleb and Samuel rode back, giving the wrathful Apaches a wide berth until they were back beside Jim Halleck. He smiled through the sweat-streaked gunsmoke that made his livid face dull and evil with its grayish coloring.

"Caleb . . . by Gawd, man, you saved the day. That was a stroke of genius." He pointed with his gore-drenched saber toward the Apaches where they had withdrawn and were holding a sullen council. "They're whipped, man. We'll herd 'em back to the reservation like a bunch of strayed sheep."

FOUR

Something in the far distance caught Caleb's keen eye. He didn't answer the major as he stared into the shimmering waves of killing heat. It had been something sharp and shiny—like the cheek piece of a bit, or perhaps the silver *concha* on a headstall. It came and went, and others like it appeared. Caleb squinted out from under the edge of his hand, and then he saw the spiral of many dust devils jerked to life by horses' hoofs and his heart sank within him. Someone was driving the Apache horses back.

"Major, there must be more Indians coming, a big band. They've rounded up the horses Sam'l an' I scattered an' are herdin' them back."

Halleck strained his eyes but couldn't see anything but the dust cloud. He shook his head uncertainly. "It couldn't be more Apaches, Caleb. Hell, they're coming up out of Mexico."

Brant spat explosively. "What in hell's that got to do with it? José Saluc's band always hightails it for Mexico because we can't chase him down there."

Halleck swore in desperation. "If it's Saluc's renegades, we're done for."

A shot rang out from the Apache camp. It fell far short of the troopers, but the triumphant screams that spanked down the hot air to the exhausted soldiers let them know that the Apaches had seen the returning horse herd. Halleck turned to his men. His frantic gaze looked for horses fresh enough to head off the Apache remuda, but he found none. His troopers, too, were badly off. He swung toward Doorn. "We've got to intercept 'em, Caleb, or, by Gawd, we're finished. We got to keep 'em from gettin' a-horseback again. It's questionable whether we can handle Saluc's band alone, but we sure as hell can't handle all of 'em."

Caleb nodded and raised his arm slowly, pointing back over the desert beyond the dismounted Apache bivouac. Halleck followed his arm and started suddenly in the saddle. Bearing down, behind the Apaches—who were too busy watching their tribesmen bringing up their horses to look behind them—and about equal distance away was a glittering line of cavalrymen riding in a long-legged lope, sabers drawn and extended. Halleck's exultant bellow brought his own troopers' attention to the soldiers riding up.

"Edmonds from Defiance, by Gawd. Relief!"

A ragged, sobbing shout went up from the agency troopers. The Apaches looked over at them in bewilderment, took their cue from the direction of the soldiers' faces, and looked behind them. It was an awful moment for them. The Fort Defiance soldiers were bearing down like demons in blue. With a ragged and useless volley of carbine fire, they tried to scatter. Halleck immediately ordered his troops to form in a large half circle and ride in. Colonel Edmonds understood and fanned his troopers out until the Apaches were completely encircled in a great cordon of blue. Caleb looked back at the Indians bringing up the stampeded horses. They had stopped stockstill.

For a long moment no one seemed to know exactly what to do. Caleb turned to Jim Halleck. "Come on, Major, there's one slim chance we can avert a real battle. Let's try it." He was riding down over the line toward the free Apaches when Halleck caught up with him.

"What's on your crazy mind, Caleb? Dammit, we'll get killed if we ride right in among 'em."

"I'm gambling that we don't . . . anyway, we'll be avenged."

Halleck tossed an odd glance at his companion but said nothing as they rode. The Apaches saw them coming. After a brief council two warriors rode out on highly bred, fat horses. Halleck eyed them ruefully and spoke out of the corner of his mouth. "Some of those California-bred horses that cowboy said they stole."

Caleb didn't answer as he reined up and held one arm aloft, palm outward in the age-old sign of peace, indicating that the man saluting bears no arms or malice. The Apaches came on at a walk, their arms extended, palms outward, too.

"José Saluc, Jim. There's your renegade."

Halleck stared glumly at the massively built, youngish warrior in the lead. "Fat lot of good it'll do me now. I'll be lucky if he doesn't use my hair for a curb strap."

"Buenas días, mi hermano."

José Saluc's beady black eyes swept over them quickly. He recognized Caleb, and inclined his head slightly. *"Buenas días, ojos claros. ¿Cómo se va?"*

For Halleck's sake, Caleb swung into English. "We were seeking the Apaches who left the reservation last night."

Saluc's impassive face turned a little so that he could see the surrounded tribesmen beyond them. "You have found them," he said simply.

"Yes, we have found them. Now they will return to the agency."

"This may be, but they will not stay. The white agent speaks with a forked tongue. He wishes my people to starve. It is said that he sells the Apache beef rations to others at a profit."

Caleb shook his head. "I don't believe that. *Jefe* Jackson is new to the West. He has much to learn, but he is not a thief."

"It may be as you say," Saluc answered dryly, "but many Apaches will starve to death while he learns. My people leave the agency in order to live. Is that a crime, that the soldiers must hunt them down?"

"No, but the Apaches must make their choice. They must either return to the reservation set aside for them, or run to Mexico as you have done."

Contempt shone in the downward pull of the renegade's face. "There is nothing but dirt and more starvation in Mexico. We would live at the agency if we knew the food would come that was promised us. It never has."

Caleb shrugged. "The Apaches can trust me."

José Saluc inclined his head again, briefly. "Yes, but it is *Jefe* Jackson we must trust, not you." Saluc remembered Doorn's recognition of him on the post and smiled slightly. "You are my friend. If you gave me your word that we would be fed like the treaty says, we would come in, but,"— the powerful shoulders rose and fell—"we do not believe the word of the agent."

Major Halleck turned to Caleb. Peace was within their grasp, and—Jackson be damned—he meant to grasp it. "Tell him you'll give him your word they'll get their beef allotment, Caleb."

Doorn turned toward the officer. "How do I know they will?"

"By Gawd, I'll personally see that they get it, if I have to club Jackson over the head to remind him when to reorder."

Saluc looked from Doorn to Halleck. "The yellow leg speaks big words. Will you give us your promise as well?"

Doorn hesitated for a fleeting second, then nodded somberly—conscious that he was promising something he had no right to promise, but making up his mind to see that something was done that would enable him to keep that promise. "I will give you my word."

José Saluc nodded brusquely. "Then it is decided, my brother. The Apaches will return to Lone Pine reservation."

Halleck wagged his head toward the surrounded Indians. "How about those?"

"They will follow José Saluc."

They did, to everyone's surprise. Saluc spoke to the sullen prisoners. His tirade was a harangue that lasted until the first stars of the summer night looked down on them. Then they agreed to return on the strength of Saluc's promise which, in turn, was based on Caleb Doorn's promise, which itself was based on nothing more solid than a scout's grim determination to see that the government kept its word to the Indians.

The wounded were loaded into the wagons, which had arrived after the fight. It was an odd sight, when the big harvest moon shone down on the arid earth and sent its benediction over the parched land, for Apaches and soldiers rode back toward the agency side-by-side. Burial parties were to follow. Caleb rode beside José Saluc, and the gaunt shadows of the long blue column, leading riderless horses, passed over them with a regular rhythm.

"If the Indians could choose an agent, you would be chosen," Saluc told Caleb.

"I am honored, José Saluc, but I am only a scout on the frontier of our nation. Agents must come from Washington."

The Apache spat. "The West needs Westerners, not Easterners. *Jefe* Jackson is a fool. You know this whether you say so or not. He is no man for an agent. If it isn't beef, it will be something else. He is treacherous, too . . . you will see."

Caleb fully agreed, but for the sake of unity he couldn't say so. He changed the subject. "The Apaches must speak to their agent only through their council. If there is trouble, don't let your young men take up arms. Let your council speak for them."

Saluc watched the eerie silhouettes arise up out of the flat ground as the agency buildings came into sight. "You fear the agent's revenge against us for leaving the reservation?"

"Not if I can get to him before he takes action."

Saluc stopped his horse and looked gravely at Caleb. "I hope there is no trouble, *mi hermano*. The next time the Apaches leave, they will never return." He nodded and turned to follow his people past the big stockade gate. The soldiers rode silently in past the guard, their recent enemies going forward like ghostly wraiths and night spirits. Only the occasional clatter of accoutrements broke the heavy silence.

Halleck mustered his men and dismissed them. A leeching weariness was rampant within him. He sagged when he turned to Caleb, who had given his own horse to Brant. "Come on, let's go nail Jackson."

Caleb nodded thoughtfully. If they didn't do it now, tired as they were, the agent might take retaliatory action against the returned rebels and undo, again, all the good they had achieved with blood and sweat.

Alger Jackson heard their reports with a complacent smile. He knew his position was secure and felt warmly comfortable after a big meal. The bloodshot eyes and gray, sagging faces before him were symbols of an inner exhaustion approaching the breaking point. "You have done a remarkable job, gentlemen. Remarkable."

Caleb frowned past the compliment. "How about the beef ration?"

Jackson put both hands, palm upward, in front of him. "It'll be along in a week or ten days. Patience, gentlemen, patience."

Halleck exploded. "Patience be damned, sir! These Indians have to eat an' we've promised them they would."

Jackson's face flushed a dark red. "You had no right to make that promise. You"—looking straight at the major—"are only the officer in charge of military patrols here at the agency, and you"—he faced Caleb with a triumphant leer—"are only a scout. A glorified squawman."

Halleck saw Caleb's face drain of color as he spoke. "But you said we were to tell you what to do in order to make this post function peaceably, just before we left."

Jackson smiled blandly. "That was true then, gentlemen, but now the Indians have been beaten and forced to return. I can take over from here on and you will revert to your old status as subordinates."

Doorn's voice was very soft. His bitterness overwhelmed him. This sneaking fool in front of him was going to make his word to the Apaches worthless. "Then you are not going to expedite the delivery of the beef?"

"No! I'll teach these savages patience if it takes every gun and every soldier in the territory!"

"Don't you have a cash fund for emergencies?"

"Of course, and it's ample to purchase local beef. But I'm going to teach these swine a lesson in hunger they'll never forget! I'll. . ."

"No you won't, Jackson!" the major exclaimed.

"By Gawd, Major Halleck, you'll go to your quarters an' consider yourself under arrest. I'll take no in-subordination from the likes of you. If necessary, I'll. . ."

"Rope it, Jackson!" Doorn's sunken eyes were baleful and ice cold. "The major isn't under arrest, an' you'll buy beef to tide over until the regular herd arrives!"

Jackson was on his feet with clenched fists. "Doorn, I'll break you, I'll. . ."

"Buy that beef, Jackson, or, by Gawd, I'll kill you!"

The awful tension in the room had reached a terrible climax of wild tempers held in restraint by the narrowest of margins. Jackson's mean features worked under the impetus of his fury. Out of the corner of his eye he saw the sagging pistol against the major's leg. It was close enough so that he could yank it out in a second. His insane hatred of the buckskin-clad scout in front of him was overpowering. With a wild, shrill oath he grabbed out the gun and swung it to bear. Doorn's worn gun leapt into his fingers like a living thing, its snout bellowing orange flame and sudden death. He thumbed a second shot, although the first had been sufficient. A rattle of running feet intermingled with the musical tinkle of spurs sounded loud in the deathly stillness, then the door was thrown violently inward and Colonel Edmonds stood framed in the doorway.

"Good Lord! What happened?"

Halleck told him in succinct sentences.

Edmonds went around the desk and looked at the dead man, picked up Halleck's gun, fired it into the log wall, and put it back in Jackson's hand. "Well, gentlemen, it was purely a case of self-defense."

He strode around in front of the desk that hid the body and looked sharply at Doorn. "By the power vested in me as military commandant of this territory, I hereby appoint you, Caleb Doorn, as acting Indian agent at Lone Pine Agency until your appointment can be confirmed through regular channels." He swung to Halleck. "Major, you'll work in collaboration with Acting Agent Doorn. And, by the way, boys, I heard part of what Jackson said as I was walking toward the office. For Gawd's sake, buy enough beef to keep the Indians on the agency, will you?"

For the first time in many days Jim Halleck felt a great load lifted from his chest. Even the weariness of his exhausted body seemed to fall away. He offered his hand in silent tribute to the colonel. Edmonds shook it in slight embarrassment, smiled, and headed for the door. "I'm goin' back to Fort Defiance, boys . . . been away too long already. Anything you need, send Sam'l over. He's the best damned chess player I've found in this hell-hole of a country in five years."

Caleb took a long soaking bath in the wooden tub he kept for that purpose. He was drowsy and his mind kept following a dim trail beyond the post toward an embattled log cabin where a thin wisp of a girl stood in the doorway. He smiled peaceably. He'd go see her the next day. As the new agent, he'd have to give her his word, too, that the Indians wouldn't molest the Callahan Ranch any more. Who knew, but what she'd want to be reassured occasionally? He dreamed blissfully of the flashing eyes and taffy hair until he almost went to sleep in the bathtub.

NIGHT OF THE
COMANCHEROS

ONE

A misty halo of evening light lay across the mountains, softening their harshness, shadowing their corners, their thrusts and lists and tumbling cañons, making them appear to be what they were not and never had been, benign and friendly. Catclaw and yucca and thorny sage grew where the soil was deepest; elsewhere annual grasses showed pale-green. Except for that late-day mistiness the mountains were hard and bleak, and, as the horseman passed down their south slope, they seemed friendly, but he was not deluded. He'd ridden these hills before. He knew how unfriendly they really were, how savagely uncompromising in blazing summer and how cruel in winter.

Far out where the land lay flat and dusty was the west Texas town of Tenawa, named for a fierce group of Comanche Indians who had once, long ago, roamed this vast, empty, and lonely land. This was cattle country, all the way from those northerly mountains to the Mexican border that followed a crooked old river in the distance east to west as far as a man could ride. It

49

was a hard land and the people who inhabited it had its mark upon them. For generations there had been wars here, first against the wild Comanches, then against marauders up out of Mexico, then the War Between the States that had ended with Texas and the Confederacy humbled, and, finally, the battles had degenerated into deadly little skirmishes, sometimes between Mexican raiders, sometimes between the hair-triggered men of converging cattle empires, and quite often simply between two men with hip-holstered six-guns who were full of the pride and the yeast of youth.

From Tenawa each spring the Texans rode forth to join big cattle drives. In the fall they returned, not as many as had earlier ridden out because some died every summer in the gunsmoke and bedlam of the wild trail towns of Kansas and Nebraska or farther north up in Montana, Wyoming, Colorado, or Utah Territory. But once a man had been "up a trail", he was never again the same. He had seen the world beyond Texas, had crossed paths with the fast men and loose women, had seen men die over the turn of a card or a mumbled slur, had weathered storms and droughts and pitch-black nights surrounded by five thousand treacherous, wicked-horned Texas longhorns. In short, he'd ridden out of Tenawa a boy and had returned a man—if he lived to return at all. The boothill cemeteries from the Canadian to the Sacramento had rows of buried Texans in them. But if he returned, he was not at all the same person as when he left.

This had happened to Buckley Baylor. He had still been called Bucky when he'd gone north the spring before. He'd been called Bucky by his mother ever since he could remember. But somewhere between the Red River and the Flint Hills of Kansas he had become simply Buck Baylor, Texas trail hand, tough, resourceful, good with gun or fists or lariat, lanky and big-boned and hard as iron. The trail did that. It separated the men from the boys. It hardened a man's resolve and it tempered his youthfulness with a rough kind of understanding and wisdom.

Buck Baylor, returning to Tenawa with a doeskin poke full of gold pieces, had served his apprenticeship. He passed down that south slope meeting the mountains as an equal, as cruel as they were, as flinty and hard and punishing, if he had to be, as any mountains, any plains, or any men in Texas.

He struck the plain and veered eastward, no longer heading for Tenawa, which had until now been his lodestar. He rode as a man will who has spent much time apart from other men. His eyes missed nothing; his body was loose over leather; his expression was relaxed. He passed along, permitting fragments of memory to hold his attention. Yonder, where gray smoke rose straight up into this ending day, was the Kilgore place. Westerly laid the blue-blur of lupine that characterized the north range of old Justin Frazier's Five-Pointed Star Ranch. On downcountry, not entirely visible yet, was the Dave Baylor Ranch; actually not much of a ranch as cow outfits went in west Texas, but it had been good to his father and his mother. It had also been good to him. He'd learned to ride there, to rope and shoot and sweat hard.

Easterly, the way he was heading now, out and around Tenawa, that stood forth upon the plain as an ugly, functional, squat old town, easterly there with the soft half-light of dusk mantling everything, was the Hardesty place. Buck was heading straight as an arrow for the Hardesty Ranch. Over the dwindling flames of a thousand campfires with the pure flare of desert behind him, or the stiff-standing ranks of north-country pines and firs, Buck Baylor had seen the smiling soft eyes and the sweetly heavy mouth of Carol Hardesty.

When other men had loped out for the border towns with a whoop and a thirst, he had pouched his wages, had laid back upon his bedroll, gazing at the vaulted skies, dreaming of this moment when he'd come riding down the land east of Tenawa. Only he'd always envisioned his triumphant returning as occurring during daylight.

But the details were unimportant; daylight or dark, it was all the same. On his right, now, Tenawa began to show lamplight. It firmed up under his gaze, looking good to him after so long an absence. There would be a lot to hear. There would be new faces, changes, and—an absence of some of the old faces. Johnny Smith, for example, would not be there, or Clyde Bailey, or Tenawa Lewis, who had been churned into jelly by sharp hoofs one night north of the Canadian when a sudden, blinding bolt of lightning had started a stampede that didn't end for seven miles.

He rode close enough to hear men hooting at one another from the saloons and the dusty roadway, to see riders loping in from the range, to feel the pull and the poignancy every man feels when he's home again after a long, perilous time in the outside world. But he kept on around town, cut the easterly trail to those outlying ranches, and came finally into the yard of Frank Hardesty's FH outfit. Dusk was down now with its sad, sad light and its gentle mood. There was a light in the house as Buck dismounted, led his animal into the barn, forked him a bait of hay, loosened his rigging, removed the headstall, then just stood there, one hand upon his saddle, breathing deeply of the hay smell, the cooling earth's unique aroma, feeling the peculiar combination of goodness and sadness a man feels after so long a time of being away.

He had no sensation of not being alone in Frank Hardesty's barn until a voice came over to him from the rearward gloom, saying, almost mournfully: "Hello, Bucky."

He turned, stiffening at this unexpected presence, seeing it move heavily out of a tie stall where the man had been collecting hens' eggs in his hat, seeing the man only as a bulky, square shape until he got close enough to the barn's front opening for that lingering late light to show him the open, rugged countenance of Carol's father.

"I saw you coming," Hardesty said. "I knew who it was. You used to come loping in, ridin' straight up like that. No one else sat their saddle quite like you did, Bucky."

Hardesty looked at the eggs in his hat. He looked at them for a long time. Buck watched him and it was not the expression he saw, because it was too dark for that. It was something else. It was the sag of his shoulders, the heavy stance, the resignation and the listlessness. He kept watching Carol's father. A knottiness began inexplicably to form in his stomach. His sixth sense told him there was something wrong here, something badly wrong.

Frank looked up. "We heard you were dead, Bucky. I don't recollect now who, but someone come a month or two back, sayin' that you'd been gunned down in Dodge City."

Buck kept still, sniffing this confusing atmosphere, trying mightily to catch some hint about what was crowding around him in the gloom with its unpleasant aura. He was a man of strong premonitions. He'd survived the treachery of lethal nights and unpredictable days because he had this ability. But it never quite told him *what* was wrong; it only warned him that *something* was wrong.

Hardesty moved over closer to the door. He looked out over the yard a moment. He looked southward toward his lighted house. He moved back again.

"You better go on home," he said softly. "Your ma'll be lookin' for you, Bucky. You go on home, an' maybe tomorrow or the next day you come on back."

Frank stepped out of the barn and started shuffling across toward the house. Buck stood a moment without moving, his premonition stronger than ever. He went over and watched Carol's father fade out in darkness over by the side of the house. He stood a long time like that, puzzled and troubled and uncertain, then he went back, bitted his animal, yanked at the latigo, led the horse out, and stepped up. He was angry now, along with being troubled. He'd known burly Frank Hardesty since he'd been a boy. Never had he been bitten off short like this before at the Hardesty place. It rankled, but it also hurt.

He reined around, his pride making his hand heavy on the reins. He loped away with his head twisted, watching the ranch house until it dropped away in the darkness. He cut along toward Tenawa, feeling fierce and disturbed. Several riders loomed ahead, swinging toward town. He made no attempt to ride around them but made them do the turning. Something black and cruel was in him, twisting his lips and darkening his eyes. Those four horsemen gave way, then reined up, looking after him. One of them said in a slightly breathless, slightly startled way: "That was Buck Baylor." Another said: "It couldn't be, Sam. He got it up in Dodge City." "Well, then, by God, it was his ghost. He passed less'n ten feet in front of me an', I'm tellin' you, boys, that was Buck Baylor. Hell, I ought to know, I grew up with him."

The full weight of darkness was down now. A sprinkling of stars cast sharp, brittle light earthward, and off in the purple night where the moon would shortly rise was a pale glow. Whereas the dusty horsemen loped along, Buck, a faint, long shadow, hurried ahead of them until, near the familiar old cut-off leading into a ranch yard, both rider and shadow slowed. Ahead, patiently standing in the faint-lighted night, were buildings. An old barn, half logs, half adobe, a rambling house with one lamp burning in the kitchen, some outbuildings, some corrals, all painfully familiar to Buck Baylor, and yet in a way not familiar, either. Change had come to the Baylor Ranch since he'd ridden out of this same yard nearly a year before. His father had always said that maintenance was the cheapest kind of repair. Yet, as he reined down by the barn, a broken corral gate laid on his left, half lost in weeds. On his right two stringers were broken off a fence and laid now where anyone passing had only to lift them back into place.

Buck turned his horse out, hung his rig by a stirrup to one of the pegs set squarely in a log upright inside the barn, stumbled over a broken pitchfork, swore, and went on out into the yard where a west Texas night lay, bland and hushed and far-reaching. He stood a while, closing out the disappointments of this homecoming, stood there breathing in the good air and letting the flood of memories sweep over him. Here he had been born; here he had grown to manhood. He had first been bucked off a horse in this yard and had fired his first six-gun right about where he now stood. Here, too, he had embarked upon his first great adventure the springtime before, nearly a year ago.

A man's roots run deep. He can be anywhere on earth, but in his quiet hours memories lying just below the surface of his thoughts come back, strong and clear. He can be old or he can be young, he never forgets.

The old house with its verandah that ran along three sides in the Mexican style, providing shade and cool-ness during the hot months, looked better to him in the moonlight than any home he'd seen since leaving here. Better even than the governor's mansion in Austin. He started toward it, walking slowly, his gaze fixed upon that orange lamp glow.

Somewhere far out a cow bawled. Overhead the moon rode along on its silent crossing and up close to the back porch of the Baylor place Buck saw the buggy seat in time to step around it, pause a moment shaking his head, beginning to feel more and more wonderment. His father never would have. . . . The back door opened scattering his thoughts, bringing his attention swiftly around.

He recognized the woman stepping out up there, remembered that little gesture of hers of flicking up her left hand, using the back of it to push away a strand of falling hair. She stooped, put a little dish down, called to a cat, gradually turning as she did this, looking first south, then west, then north.

Her voice stopped in mid-breath; her gaze lay fully upon a lank man's rough silhouette in the northward night.

Buck said, "Hello, Ma."

For a long time the elderly woman stood without moving, without seeming even to breathe. "Is that you, Bucky?"

"Yes, Ma, it's me. I just rode in a few minutes ago."

She became unsteady there on the porch, put out a hand to the nearest upright and waited for Buck to step in closer. But she was a Texas woman with all the toughness, the resiliency of her kind; she recovered gradually, pushed back a loose strand of hair, picked up a corner of her apron and automatically wiped both hands on this, then said—"Come on, Son, you'll be hungry."—and led the way indoors.

TWO

Buck drank coffee, ignored the food, and listened to his mother's flat recital, his wonderment turning to numb incredulity, to near disbelief. The worst things in life frequently happen to a man gradually, so that he assesses them slowly. When they're thrown against him unexpectedly, he knows a kind of inner revolt, a refusal, at first, to accept them or believe them. Buck sat there now, listening, watching his mother at the stove, feeling something draining out of him, leaving his body all loose and unresponding.

"They came about four months ago. Some say they came up out of Mexico. I don't know. All I can tell you is what's happened since. They rode into the yard one morning. I was in the chicken house after the eggs. I heard them ride in, but I thought it was only Justin with some of his men, or one of the other neighbors, so I didn't come out. Not until I heard the gunshot . . . I ran out then, Bucky. Your father lay there dead. Dead in his own yard. I don't know what was said. I only know he was lying there on his back . . . dead."

For a while the only sound in that warmly lighted kitchen was of sizzling meat frying.

"Did you see any of them, Ma?"

"Two. As they rode off, two of them turned and looked back when I ran out of the hen house."

"Recognize them?"

Buck's mother shook her head. She did not face around toward him. "Not then, I didn't. They were total strangers. Later, when we buried your pa, Bucky, I saw those two in Tenawa in front of the Lone Star. They were leaning there, half smiling, Son, as the funeral procession went along through town to the burial ground. I recognized them, then. I told Frank and Justin those two were the men."

"What did Hardesty and Frazier say?"

Buck's mother turned finally, looked squarely at her son from the same dead-level light-blue eyes Buck also had, and she said: "Nothing, Son. Nothing at all. That's the way it's been ever since. Nobody says anything."

She went silent. For a long time the kitchen, the entire house, was absolutely still. Eventually she turned, nodded mechanically at the table with her face in shadows, and said: "Eat, Bucky, remember what your pa used to say? A man that won't eat hearty won't amount to much." She kept faced around but did not look at Buck, looked everywhere in her kitchen but at him.

He didn't eat. He mechanically drank black coffee, but not even very much of this, and somewhat later he walked out of the house into the moon-washed quiet night, came upon that old buggy seat again, and sank down upon it.

There is rarely the closeness between father and son

59

as between mother and son, yet there is something men can share that excludes women entirely. Buck went slowly down the years to those brief, bright moments. He recalled his father's approving smile and his bleakly disapproving scowl. He recalled Dave Baylor's big, rough hand lying gently upon his shoulder, and he also remembered it across the seat of his britches.

He knew his father as a good man, an honest, sincere Texan with a strong heart and a sympathetic streak in him as wide as the Río Grande. He had not been truculent, although he'd had his share of fights. Perhaps most significant of all, Dave Baylor's neighbors had liked him, not for two years or three years, but for the full thirty years he'd lived on this same ranch, and that, Buck concluded, was the best recommendation of a man anyone could ask.

"You'd best come in now, Son," his mother called from the porch. "I fixed your room."

He stood up, walked to the verandah, and halted there. "I want you to tell me more about those men," he said. "Why don't the others go after them? I don't understand, Ma. Tenawa's a tough town."

"Son," his mother said softly from the porch shadows, "the man who leads them . . . his name is Brownell . . . Cleve Brownell . . . has money. Money is power, Bucky. Since the war we in Texas have seen little enough hard money. It'll buy a lot of things."

"You're sayin' this Brownell's bought the town? I can't believe that, Ma. Why, old man Frazier and Frank Hardesty. . ." Buck stopped speaking. Something painful had passed over his mother's face like a shadow.

He stood a moment, looking ahead. Somewhere inside his brain that warning premonition jangled.

"Ma, I was over at Hardesty's tonight."

Her eyes lifted, ran over Buck's face, and swiftly fell.

"Frank . . . acted odd. He told me to come back in a day or two."

"Well," his mother said heavily, "he wouldn't want to be the one. I'm your mother, Buckley, and I don't want to be the one, either. Least of all me, for the love of God."

"What are you talking about?"

"Go to bed, Son," his mother said solemnly. "Get some rest. We'll talk tomorrow."

"Listen, Ma, I want to know right now . . . not tomorrow. What is it no one wants to tell me?"

His mother went to a wicker-bottom porch chair and sank down. She had an old shawl that she now drew closer about both shoulders, although the night was warm. She rocked a little, looking straight out, and she said: "I heard a rumor, Bucky. Someone came back from the drives and had word of you bein' killed up in Kansas." She raised her eyes to him, caressing him this way. "You're young. You can't know what it is like, losing both the people you've always lived for, in one summer. You wish to die and you don't die, so you just keep doing routine things, waiting. I don't know what for, but you just keep waiting."

Buck stepped up, leaned upon a verandah post, and waited. His mother did nothing hastily. She never had. She was a reflective person and she put her great store in her Bible. She interpreted things in the light of the

Scriptures. He knew these things, so he stood waiting. She spoke again, her tone fading out a little, turning flat again, empty-sounding, as though she were reciting one thing and thinking another.

"Brownell took Carol, Son. He took her the first month after he came to Tenawa. The month after he killed your pa . . . or had his men kill your pa."

Buckley felt for the bench nearby, and eased down upon it.

"He never married her and after a while she went to work in the Lone Star. Last month she left town on the westbound stage." His mother's toneless voice ceased, then started up again. "Frank Hardesty didn't want to tell you, Son. Now do you see? I didn't want to tell you, either. You've just come back from the grave, Buckley. Now you'll go back to it. Son, Cleve Brownell has been the cause of four deaths in Tenawa. You'll be the fifth."

They sat on, still and silent for a long, long time, neither of them seeing the other, neither of them thinking the same thoughts, the vault of heaven with its eternal promise of a new dawn, of a new life, serenely overhead. The myriad little cold-flickering stars were like urchin children of the yellowish old moon, scattered at random across an unrelieved sky of enameled purple.

"Go to bed, Son," Mahalia Baylor said once, quietly. "Go to bed and tomorrow we'll talk about leaving."

Buck looked over. "Leaving?"

"I've been thinking that for some time now. You coming back makes it seem better even than it seemed when I thought I was the only one of us left. We'll leave the Tenawa country, Son. I've got kin in Virginia, the Buckleys, Son, my brothers' families. We'll go back to Virginia, you and me." Mahalia looked to see how her son was taking this. She could make out no expression at all in the gloom, only the faint outline of a high cheekboned, rugged face. The night played a cruel trick on Mahalia. It made Buck's features identical with those of his dead father. A knife twisted in her heart. She caught her breath and held it, hard, then let it slowly out.

"You'll be killed, Son. There are too many of them. Brownell won't wait. As soon as he hears Dave Baylor's boy is back . . . Carol Hardesty's promised is back . . . he'll send those men out to find you." Mahalia held her shawl with both work-worn hands, drawing it still closer. "He'll have to do that, Son. He'll have to."

Buck stood up. "You got any whiskey in the house?" he asked.

Mahalia shook her head.

Buck went to the very edge of the porch and halted there, looking over the pewter yard. When he spoke, his voice was dull.

"I saved my pay. I got the buckskin pouch in my pocket right now. I rode over to show Carol." He whipped around, his face stricken, his eyes nearly black with the hurt of all this. "What kind of a man has Frank Hardesty turned out to be?" he fiercely demanded.

"She was of age, Son. Little Carol went with him of her own free will."

"That's a lie!" he raged. "She wrote me a letter last spring. I got it up in Dodge City. She wanted me to hurry back."

"Brownell didn't come until mid-summer, Son," reminded his mother.

"But, Frank . . . ?"

"I just told you, Bucky. Little Carol went of her own free will. Frank tried. I know for a fact that he tried. He even threatened to lock her in the house." Mahalia paused. She rocked her chair back and forth several times. "Afterward, Frank went to see her, to fetch her back home. Doc Barnes sent for Frank. Carol tried to kill herself. Frank wanted to take her home. She wouldn't go. She went to work in the Lone Star Saloon for Charley Gifford. Charley told Frank he'd watch over her. He did. He did it so well she got on the westbound coach one day not too long ago, and just disappeared."

"And Frank," said Buck bitterly, nearly choking, "you know what he was doin' when I rode in over there tonight? Gatherin' god-damned eggs in his hat in the barn. He didn't even have on a gun."

"Don't blaspheme, Son. I don't like it and you know your pa wouldn't have liked it."

"I'll blaspheme," raged Buck. "I'll damned well blaspheme. Y'all sittin' around here . . . Frank not even goin' after this Brownell."

"Buckley, stop it. Listen to me. Carol's mother's down in bed with it. How would it help now if Frank Hardesty got himself killed goin' up against Cleve Brownell's gunfighters? Tell me how that would help? Or you . . . riding into Tenawa for your pa? How would that help you or your dead pa . . . or me?"

Mahalia got up, stood away from the rocking chair, still clutching the old shawl. "Son, we've got to leave here. We've got to get away tomorrow, no later than the day after. Even if you don't get yourself killed, believe me, Brownell will hear that you're back and he'll have you killed."

Buckley turned away again, stood tall and thinned-down and rock-like with faint moonlight across his evenly sun-layered face. He said in an altered, soft, and very quiet voice: "No, Ma, we're not leaving."

He stepped down off the porch, went pacing toward the barn, and disappeared from his mother's sight in there. A little later she heard a horse walk out into the westerly night from the barn's rear opening, walk perhaps a hundred yards before it broke over into a long lope, heading outward bound into the night.

Mahalia returned to the rocker, sat down, and began moving back and forth, back and forth, the only audible sound after that galloping horse was lost northward, the cadenced grind of chair rockers over scuffed verandah planking.

Mahalia was a praying woman, yet she could not pray now. She was too full of agony. Why had the Lord sent her boy back this night at all? Why hadn't He let Bucky stay in that rumored grave in Kansas? At least, that way she could have eventually come to live with her grief. This way, she would have very shortly now to learn how to grieve all over again. The Lord's way was hard, and Mahalia Baylor just could not bring herself to pray. Just could not.

THREE

It was very late when the shadowy horseman entered Justin Frazier's ranch yard, riding slowly. He passed in front of the bunkhouse, the barn, the network of pole corrals, and alighted by the house. Around back, a dog began to bark furiously, shattering the stillness with his racket.

For a little while the only sound was of that dog, then a sleep-roughened voice bellowed for the dog to be quiet. But this seemed only to aggravate the animal. Buck could hear it lunging against the restraint of a chain as he moved along in front of the house, the scent of honeysuckle nearly overpowering here, where tended vines rose up in profusion to wrap themselves around verandah uprights.

In the back of Justin Frazier's rambling ranch house that sleepy voice turned fully, angrily awake. It swore at the dog, then it went silent. Buckley raised one fist, rolled his knuckles loudly across the massive oaken front door, and stepped clear, waiting.

For a long time there was no sound from within,

only the diminishing growls of the chained dog. Buck thought once he'd heard padding big feet on the other side of the door, but they stopped.

"Who is it . . . out there?" a deep voice inquired. "What do you want?"

Buck looked at the door, running something through his mind. Justin Frazier, one of the biggest cowmen in the Tenawa country with five tough riders and a reputation for courage, was standing behind a door calling out. This did not square with the memory Buck had of old Justin, the durable widower with one gangling, pigtailed child, a daughter named Kathleen, who looked more boy than girl.

"Who is it. Dammit, speak up out there!"

Buck spoke up. "I just rode over from the Baylor place," he said. "I'd like a word with you, Mister Frazier."

"Step up where I can get a look at you," ordered the unseen cowman. "Up closer to the door."

Buckley stepped right up. He hooked both thumbs in his shell belt, feeling oddly self-conscious because he knew old Justin's hazel eye was squinting at him through the long-unused gun-slot in the door. He heard the older man let out a gasp, then the door swung open.

"Good God, boy!" exploded Frazier. "Buckley Baylor."

Buck nodded. He was unsmiling. "Since when have you taken to hiding behind doors?" he asked, making no move to enter the house although the tousled older man, standing there in his nightshirt with a Winchester in one hand, stepped back for him to do so. "You've changed, Mister Frazier."

The old cowman gaped and scarcely heard. He was very obviously upset and incredulous at the identity of his midnight visitor. "Buckley! Son, we heard you were dead."

"I know. I've heard that, too. Killed up in Dodge City."

"Yes. Come in, boy, come in."

Buck did not move. "I came over to ask you some questions, Mister Frazier."

"All right, son. But come in, come in."

"No. I want you to tell me how it is that none of you other cowmen has done anything about this Brownell."

Raw-boned old Justin Frazier's slatey eyes slowly dimmed, gradually blanked over. He bent to put aside his carbine and did not immediately thereafter straighten up. He set the Winchester just so, moved it a little, and set it just so again.

"You've heard about your pa, son. I'm dead sorry about that. Everyone is, Bucky. Real sorry."

"Just not sorry enough, though. Is that it, Mister Frazier?"

Old Frazier drew upright. He was nearly a foot wider but not one inch taller than Buck Baylor. All the surprise and enthusiastic pleasure were wiped from his face now. "You've been gone a spell," he said in a quieter tone. "You don't know how things are, Buckley."

Buckley agreed with this. "No, I don't. That's why I rode over here . . . to find out."

"Son, leave it be."

Buck wagged his head, but not in disagreement particularly, rather in perplexed disappointment. "You've changed," he said. "Mister Frazier, my pa used to say

68

you were all wool an' a yard wide. He'd told me many a time Justin Frazier's a man to ride the rim rocks with."

"Buckley, your pa's dead. He's been dead months now. Listen to me, son, you an' Kathleen grew up together. You were like one of my own, so let me talk to you like a father. I know how you feel. I can read it in your eyes. But, Buckley, don't get yourself killed over something that's done and buried. Son, think of your ma."

"And Carol Hardesty, Mister Frazier. I'm thinking of her, too." Buck's pale gaze turned hard. It punished the older man with its bleakness and its thickening contempt. "Suppose that had been Kathy instead of Carol. Would you still hide behind your door?"

Old Frazier's square jaw snapped closed. His eyes blazed with a sudden hot brightness. "Get on your horse and get to hell off my land, Buckley. Go on now . . . get!"

Buck did not move but the outer corners of his lips pulled down a little. "You want to try running me off?" he softly asked. "Let me tell you something, Mister Frazier. That wasn't all rumor you heard about me getting shot up in Dodge City. A pardner of mine and I shot it out with four broncho east Texans. I got one through the lung. That's probably where the rumor started about me being dead. But those four east Texas boys got killed, got out-drawn and out-gunned. You still want to try me, Mister Frazier?"

The two stood in the shank of the night, staring at one another. Finally Justin Frazier stepped through the door, softly closed it behind him, and said: "Buckley, your odds are a heap bigger this time. Brownell's got ten men. They're never all at the same place at the same time. I've heard it said he'll bring twenty more to Tenawa if he has to. You don't stand the chance of a prayer in hell, so get that through your bull-headed skull. Not a chance at all. If you're wise, you'll load your ma into a wagon and get out. Keep goin' until you're plumb out of Texas."

Buckley said flatly: "You're yellow, Mister Frazier. I wish my pa could hear you right now. It'd make him sick to his stomach. You're as yellow as a. . . ."

Frazier swung. Buck saw it coming, blocked the punch, and gave the older man a rough shove. "I guess I made a wrong guess," he growled as Frazier righted himself, his back against the house. "I guess I should have said you've got courage enough to fight your friends but not enough to fight your enemies."

Frazier breathed heavily. "Brownell's no enemy of mine. He wouldn't be yours, either, if you'd get some sense."

Buck stood still, letting the older man say all his anger made him say. For a moment he simply gazed at Frazier, then he said, speaking very slowly and deliberately: "I didn't know a person could be so wrong about another person. I've known you all my life and my pa before me knew you. Yet, tonight, you've turned out to be nothing at all like we've always thought."

Frazier checked himself, throttled his anger, and ran a hand through his hair. In a different manner, looking more troubled than Buck had ever seen him look before, he stepped away from the house, stepped up close, and looked hard at young Baylor.

"Just for a minute listen to me, Buckley. Just for a

moment forget your pa and Frank's daughter and let me give you some facts. This country's been starvin' since the war. Folks hereabouts have actually been without enough to eat, except for cattle. Now I'm not saying I agree with what Brownell's doing. I don't agree with it. But he's helpin' folks hereabouts."

"How? What exactly is he doing?"

"He . . . brings . . . good Mex cattle over the line, lines up local cowmen to take 'em on shares or trail 'em north to Dodge or some other railhead, and sell 'em." Frazier paused, studied young Baylor's face, then went on. "He's put money into folks' pockets and food into their mouths. He's put life back into Tenawa."

"All those men who work for him . . . they steal the Mex cattle and fetch 'em over the line. Y'all don't have any hand in the rustling?"

"No. He does it all. When they're delivered here on the range, he comes out an' makes a deal with us. As far as we know, the critters are legally his."

"Except that you know a damned sight better, Mister Frazier."

Old Justin lifted his shoulders and let them fall. He stood mute, waiting for Buck's reaction to all this.

Buck's brows rolled up in a puzzled frown. "If it's all as clean as you say, why did Brownell have my pa killed?"

But Frazier, if he knew the answer to this, would not comment. He only shook his head.

"And if Brownell's such a benefactor, Mister Frazier, what about Carol Hardesty?"

"I don't know anything about that, Buckley."

"You've got ears, haven't you, and eyes? You and my pa and Frank used to be good friends. Now . . . there's only you. By the way, you never answered me . . . suppose it had been Kathy instead of Carol?"

Frazier's jaw locked, his eyes smoldered. "It wasn't," he snapped. "It wasn't an' that's all there is to it."

Buck's blue gaze turned hard, turned cruel. "I'm going to meet this Cleve Brownell. I always wanted to get a long look at a real cow thief."

"He'll kill you."

"Naw. A man who sends gunmen to do his killing won't kill anyone, Mister Frazier. Not by himself he won't. And that's where I've got an advantage, you see, because *I will*."

"Let me give you a little advice, Buckley. Be out of the Tenawa country by tomorrow night."

"Why? You going to run over right quick and tell Brownell I'm out to kill him?"

"I won't have to tell him a thing. He'll know by morning who you are. After that . . . you can get it anytime. But if you'll give me your word you'll leave, I'll go see him in the morning. I'll ask him to give you until tomorrow night."

Buck stepped off the porch, went out to his horse, and leaned there briefly before mounting. "You make me want to throw up!" he exclaimed. "God, Mister Frazier, I've had three things hit me harder today than anythin' ever before hit me in my life. Pa's murder, Carol, and now you. You . . . turnin' out to be something too low to wear pants and walk upright." He mounted, shortened his reins, and put a final look upon the older man, standing there in his nightshirt. "Go on back to bed and have a good sleep. Dream of little Carol and my pa and the others Brownell's ruined."

Buck spun his horse and loped out of the yard. As he passed the Texas Star bunkhouse, he looked over at it. Frazier used to employ local riders. Buck wondered if he still did, and which local men, who knew what was going on, would work for him?

He didn't return home or go into town. He cut out northeasterly, around Tenawa, where a few lights still flickered, loped steadily along to the main gate of the Kilgore place. It was now morning, but the sun would not arise for another two hours at the least. It was getting close to the hour when lights would be coming on again, though, in kitchens and cook shacks and bunkhouses as ranchers and their hired hands arose to begin the new day's work.

Wyatt Kilgore, Buck's father used to say, was as stubborn as a horse mule, as tough as a boiled owl, and as cantankerous as a rutting buck. He was not a large man, as Buck remembered him, but he was reputedly very fast with a gun. There was even talk, for a while, that Wyatt had been an outlaw. But if that were so, it would have had to have been at least thirty years back, because, ever since Buck could remember, he'd been building up and operating his Fishhook outfit northeast of Tenawa.

Riding into the Fishhook yard now, Buck thought that this was not going to be a pleasant meeting either way. But he was beginning to firm up an idea in his mind, and he wanted to hear Kilgore's side of this Brownell thing exactly as he'd heard Justin Frazier's.

When a man was getting set to brace a nest of rattlesnakes, the more he could learn the better, even if he jeopardized himself as he'd just done over at Frazier's Texas Star, in order to learn what he had to know.

He dismounted, looped his reins through a stud ring, and straightened around at the precise moment someone over in the Fishhook bunkhouse lighted a coal-oil lamp.

A tall man stepped forth from that yonder building with boots in his hand. He went two or three steps, sat down, lifted a leg, and was in the act of tugging on a boot when he suddenly froze, motionless, staring over where Buck stood in sooty gloom by Wyatt Kilgore's residence.

Buck sensed rather than saw the cowboy's abrupt alertness, his sudden wariness and antagonism. "You, there," the cowboy called out. "You, over there by the house . . . what you doin' slippin' around here in the dark?"

The man got up and started over the yard. He was still holding a boot in one hand. Buck, under different circumstances, might have smiled or even laughed at this limping, lank figure of a man with sleep-puffy eyes and a soiled undershirt walking so belligerently forward. Tonight was, however, the time in Buckley Baylor's life when humor was furthest from him.

The cowboy halted three feet away. He was Buck's equal in height but he had easily a twenty-pound advantage. His disadvantage was simply that, while he was truculent, he was not deadly, and this night Buck was. Without a word Buck sprang in, fired a sledgehammer blow, and Wyatt Kilgore's cowboy fell like a pole-axed steer.

FOUR

The owner of Fishhook opened the door in response to Buck's knocking. He was freshly shaved and cleanly attired, and he was also scowling. No one ever knocked on the main house front door unless he was a stranger, and at four o'clock in the morning wispy, dark, and vinegary Wyatt Kilgore could not imagine who would be out there.

He squinted up into Buck's face, but if he was astonished at the identity of his caller, Wyatt Kilgore never showed it. He did, however, hang fire a second or two over his greeting, then all he said was: "Come in, Buck. You're in time for breakfast."

Buck stepped into Kilgore's parlor, which was a veritable pack rat's nest of disorder. Kilgore was a lifelong bachelor, and he was also something else, a working cowman by trade and choice. If something did not fit into his pattern of cow-camp existence, he ignored it. That went for such minor things as dust and house furniture and women.

He closed the door after Buckley, passed around

him, and halted, looking up, his dark, forthright gaze flinty, appraising, and unreadable. Without wasting a single word Kilgore said: "All right, Buck, from the looks of you, I'd guess you just rode in tonight."

"That's right, Wyatt."

"And I can see the rest of it in your face. But why ride over here and pick on me?"

"You were my second choice."

Kilgore's eyes moved a little. "Yeah," he muttered dryly. "I can imagine who your first choice was. Well, did you like what you found at Texas Star?"

"No, sir."

"An' what makes you think you'll find anything different at Fishhook?"

"I don't hardly know what to think, Wyatt. I never thought I'd find old Justin changed like he is."

Kilgore said a coarse word and twisted his face. "He hasn't changed, Buck. I know how you an' your pa thought he was honest and tough and neighborly. Well, it wasn't none of my affair, but I've known a lot of Justin Fraziers in my time. I can smell opportunists a long ways off. The trouble is, boy, you could live next to one for a hundred years, and, unless something like Brownell happened to a country, folks would never know what's really inside the Justin Fraziers of this world."

"It was pretty hard to take."

Men clumped along outside the house. One of them let off a sharp little yelp. There was the quick slam of hurrying boot steps toward the front of Kilgore's house, then voices raised in puzzlement. Kilgore's head went up. He looked past Buck and listened.

"Now what the hell?" he growled.

"I knocked out one of your riders, Wyatt," said Buck.

"You what?"

"I was tyin' up outside. He came across the yard at me."

"Well, dammit, he had the right." Kilgore stopped speaking, swung past, and threw open the front door. He didn't go over where a little cluster of men was. He only stared out. When he saw the other cowboys supporting a groggy man, he called: "Go on in and eat! Is that you, Sam, staggerin' around? Well, you tell the cook to pour a little brandy in your coffee. I'll be along directly."

Kilgore closed the door, put his back to it, and levelly stared over at Buck for a while, looking but saying nothing. Finally he pushed forward, strolled to a chair, perched upon an arm of it, and fixed Buck with a severe look.

"I understand how you feel, findin' out about Justin like you did. But don't come around here making trouble, Buck, or you'll regret it."

"It wasn't only Justin. I was over at Frank Hardesty's tonight. Also, I was home."

Kilgore's gaze dropped; his worn, weathered countenance became morose. After a time he said quietly: "Then I reckon you know all of it. It's damned dirty business. Damned dirty."

"Wyatt, why did he have my pa killed?"

"Your pa wasn't the only one, Buck. There have been others. It's not over with yet, this bushwhackin'. I grew an eye in the back of my head six months ago."

"Why, Wyatt?"

Kilgore looked up swiftly as a man wearing a flour-sack apron poked his balding head through a doorway. "Feed 'em," he growled. "I'll be along directly. Tell 'em to hang around outside when they're finished." The bald head disappeared and Kilgore returned his attention to Buck. "You want to know why?" he said candidly. "I'll tell you, Buck. Because your pa and a few others were secretly organizing the local folks against Brownell. That's why. You see, not everyone around here believes it's better to be a live coward than a dead hero. Your pa was one who didn't . . . so he died in his yard. Like I said, there were others. Your pa wasn't the only one."

"And you, Wyatt?"

Kilgore raised a rough hand and inspected it. "Let me tell you something," he said, speaking slowly. "Brownell's got spies in just about every bunkhouse, Buck. If you'd come around to question me after being back a week or so, I wouldn't have told you this much. He's got a way of buyin' folks . . . dead pa or no dead pa."

Buck went to a chair, pushed aside some papers, and eased down. The big room where these two sat in predawn gloom was quiet, but beyond a closed door in the west wall came sounds of men eating and talking.

"Where do you stand, Wyatt?" he asked after a time, then didn't give Kilgore time to answer, but shook his head and muttered: "How could people change so fast. What's come over Tenawa?"

"I already told you people don't change, they just become outwardly what they always have been inwardly. As for where I stand. . ."

"Yes?"

Kilgore kicked his leg back and forth. He studied Buck's face minutely. He was teetering on the verge of making a statement. Buck could see that. He could also see the dark blood surge into Kilgore's swarthy face.

"I stand against murder and rustling, but not out loud in public, Buck, and, if you're wise, you won't either." Kilgore got up off his chair. He turned business-like and brisk, but his eyes remained on Buck in that hooded, appraising way. "Go on home. Stay around the house today. Don't ask a lot of tomfool questions now. Just do as I say."

Buck also stood up. He considered the shorter, wispier man over an interval of full silence. Kilgore was telling him something, not in words or even in actions, but by his careful, forthright gaze. He nodded, stepping over to the door.

"I'll be home all day, Wyatt," he said. He opened the door, paused, and added: "Tell that cowboy I hit I'm sorry about that. It's been a long night. A feller can keep things bottled up inside him just so long."

Wyatt Kilgore gently shook his head. He made that twisted expression again. He said quietly: "No, that one deserves no apology. Like I told you, Buck . . . we got 'em in our bunkhouses, too."

Kilgore closed the door behind Buck. Outside, the first daylight streaks were yellowing an otherwise murky world. Not too far out a coyote made his mournful cry at a fading old moon, and across the Fishhook yard horses in a pole corral nickered for their breakfast.

Buck faced the new day warily. He made a big

three-quarter circle on the way back, partly because he didn't wish to be seen, partly because he wanted to think. By the time he'd gone wide around Frazier's place, had angled southward until his own place was distantly in sight, the morning was as yellow as new gold. With mounting heat upon him he began to feel the bone weariness, turning his body all loose and sagging. He came down into his own yard riding like that, reined over to the barn, stepped tiredly down, and trudged ahead to put up his horse.

A man steeped in personal troubles is rarely alert, especially if he's been hit with just about everything heartbreaking in a matter of hours. That was the way Buck now was, walking ahead of his animal, tired and benumbed and stolid, actually feeling hardly anything at all. He walked into the barn, began off-saddling, and didn't see that he was not alone until he twisted to heave his rig up by the stirrup onto its peg. There were two men leaning half in shadow across the barn calmly watching him. Buck's stirrup found the peg, weight left him as he stood there like that, both arms high upon the saddle, both eyes widened with surprise. The saddle hung where he'd meant to hang it.

"That's just right," one of those shadowy men said. "Keep your arms up like that, cowboy. That's just right."

Neither of these men had drawn a gun but both were armed and both were clearly capable men. One of them pushed up lazily and strolled over, plucked away Buck's sidearm, and carelessly tossed it into an empty manger. This man stood off a few feet and smiled. He was a little older than Buck and had a noticeable knife scar, like a crescent, on his chin. He was shorter and less durable-looking than the other man, who remained over against the far wall, blank-faced and still, but he had a look to him that went with gunmen, a kind of confident, arrogant, easy-and-relaxed look, and he kept right on smiling at Buck.

"You're pretty active," this smaller man said, through that genial smile. "You cover a heap of territory in one night, cowboy. You ask a lot of questions, too, and, while there ain't no law against askin', there's a new law hereabouts against answerin'."

Now the tougher of these two came forward. He was a man in his forties. He had not recently shaved and his jaw overbalanced the rest of his face. He had little muddy eyes and a mouthful of big square teeth. He halted, wide-legged, put his muddy glance fully upon Buck, and said: "Walk, cowboy. Head out o' here and make for the house." He paused, then growled: "Don't do nothin' silly. Just walk along like your ma wants to see you, like she wants to wipe her little boy's nose." He jerked his head.

Buck started out of the barn. Outside, bright sunlight struck quickly into his face. He squinted and walked on. The two strangers were behind him, neither of them saying anything, both of them moving confidently toward the house.

Buck halted with one foot on the verandah, twisted, and said: "Have you been in this house?"

The short man with the crescent-scar answered. His stolid, hulking companion only scowled. "Yeah we been in the house. Fact is, cowboy, we got a friend waitin' in there right now with your ma and that other feller."

Buck turned more. "What other feller?" he asked.

The gunman shrugged. "Damned if I know," he said genially. "He was here talkin' to your ma when we rode in. Said he was travelin' through. One thing's sure . . . your ma sure don't know him."

The stolid man said in a rumbling growl. "Too much talkin'. Go on in, cowboy."

Buck didn't have to open the door. It was opened for him by another rough-looking man. Across the room stood Mahalia, her face white from lips to hairline, her eyes dark with fear.

There was a darkly dressed man standing beside Mahalia. He and Buck exchanged a quick, strong look, then the man within the house said to Buck's captors: "Give you any trouble?"

"Naw. He come along meek as Moses. Real co-operatin' feller, this Baylor boy. Just like they said in town . . . quiet sort of feller, for all his size and heft."

The stranger standing facing Buck had sharp features and a long, lantern jaw. His mouth was lipless and his eyes were a peculiar, smoky shade of green. He had a six-gun in his hip holster and he also had one in his right fist. This second gun had come from the emptied holster of the big darkly dressed man over by Mahalia.

Those three strangers concentrated on Buck. Two stood a little to one side of him, the green-eyed man directly in front. He said: "Cowboy, you're gettin off easy. Too easy, to my way of thinkin'." He put the six-gun aside, drew a pair of doeskin roping gloves from his belt, and began carefully to draw them over his two big hands. He looked cruel, more cruel even than the big-jawed, stolid man. "You're goin' to get a little lesson, cowboy, an', if you got the brains God gave a goose, after it's over, you'll saddle up an' ride on. But you'll go alone. Your ma'll stay behind just in case, after you're out of the country, you get any big ideas o' comin' back with the law."

The green-eyed man nodded. Those two companions of his jumped in, caught Buck's arms, and pinioned them. Mahalia made an audible moan. The unarmed man beside her put forth a hand. When she would have moved forward, he restrained her. The green-eyed man finished with his doeskin gloves. He looked around, saying: "That's right, stranger. Don't let her do anythin' silly. You know, women break up a lot easier'n men. An' one more thing, stranger. Watch how this is done, an', when you ride out o' here, think on it a little because we don't want no outsiders in the Tenawa country."

He gave Buck no warning at all. He was still standing there with his head turned when he lashed out with the first ripping blow. It struck Buck's soft parts, the gloved fist sinking to the wrist. Buck gasped and tried to wrench away. The other two men held him. It was not easy because he was a powerful man, but they hung on doggedly as the force of those sledging blows continued. They did not have an easy time of it until Buck began to sag and aimlessly twist and turn. By then, blood was running past his lips and he blessedly did not feel the full impact of those strikes.

FIVE

It was early afternoon when Buck opened his eyes. He was in his own room, the house was utterly quiet, and standing with his back to Buck, his solemn, sundarkened face looking out a little window, was the man in black shirt and black trousers. He heard Buck move on the bed and turned. He was wearing a tight, mirthless, small smile.

"Well, now," he softly drawled. "You all got a nice country hereabouts, Buckley, except for the folks in it. How do you feel?"

"Like a herd of buffalo ran over me and the last one wiped his feet. Milt, it's good to see you. When I walked in an' saw you over there with my mother, you could've knocked me over with a feather."

"Well, hell," said the man called Milt. "You invited me down to visit you after that scrap we got into up at Dodge. An' you know me, pardner. Where there's free food and free lodgin', that's where I head after the drives are over."

Milt turned fully away from the window. He crossed

powerful arms over a deep chest and considered Buck's battered face and purple body. "Your friends play rough over here in west Texas, pardner. Mind tellin' me what that was all about?"

Buck moved, winced, and lay still. He considered the closed door of his room. He also considered the low, familiar ceiling. He began to talk, to recite the things he knew and the things he thought he knew. When he finished, a half hour later, the man called Milt sat down upon a little chair, fished out a tobacco sack, and began frowningly to concentrate upon building a smoke. After he had this lit, he dropped his serene, forthright gaze upon Buck in his bed, and said: "About that advice those boys gave you . . . you going to take it?"

Buck looked steadily over at Milt.

The latter, after a long drag off his cigarette, said: "No? Well, I didn't expect you to." He sighed, viewed the ragged tip of his cigarette, flicked off a flake of ash, and spoke again. "All right. Only I been talkin' to your ma while we sat around here waitin' for you to come to. This isn't goin' to be like buckin' those tigers up in Dodge. You know that, don't you?"

Buck nodded, gingerly probed his middle, and muttered: "That green-eyed one packs a wallop like an Army mule."

Milt eased back in the chair, looking skeptical. "Oh, I don't know about that," he said casually. "I watched him pretty close, and, you know, I think I can hit twice as hard." Milt, seeing Buck's caustic look, smiled a little. "Don't fret, Bucky, don't fret. Our turn'll come, an' you know how I am . . . sort of lazy and easy-goin' and sort of watchful-like. Well, I made a pretty good study of those boys while they were workin' you over, an' I got an idea I can take the three of 'em at the same time."

"Milt," growled Buck. "You had a pretty good opportunity this morning."

"Naw. You're just feelin' a little disgruntled now, when you say something like that. Think on it, Buck. They had my gun. I rode in here, and, before I knew it, they had me. They also out-numbered me three to one, with pistols. And to clinch it, pardner, there was your ma." Milt sadly shook his head, but his eyes slyly twinkled. "Just too big a stacked deck. But like I said, our turn'll. . ."

"Riders," snapped Buck, breaking over Milt's easy drawl. "Milt, go get Ma." He tried to sit up, wobbled, gasped, and sank back down. "Get me a gun. Don't let 'em in."

Big Milt came off that chair with the lithe grace of a panther. He didn't look fast or graceful or even quick-witted, but he was all three, and, more than that, beneath his bantering manner was a shrewdness and a hardness equal to any.

Buck watched him pass out of the room. Later, he heard Milt's deep voice speaking out in the parlor. He also heard his mother's replies, but he could distinguish nothing these two threw back and forth at one another. Then he heard a door open. Men's spurs rang as Buck listened. There was a little, hard run of quick talk that sounded blunt and unfriendly, and afterward the solid tramp of someone coming.

He thought this could be other Brownell men and

looked frantically for something that would serve as a
weapon. He was still looking when Wyatt Kilgore
stepped in, halted, and ran his dark, brittle glance up
Buck and down him. Wyatt had a shot-loaded quirt
dangling from one wrist and he had not removed the
dusty, curved Stetson on his matt of crinkly black hair.

"Well, well," he said from the doorway. "I reckon I
didn't give you such good advice, after all . . . tellin'
you to hightail it for home. How bad off are you?"

"I'll live," replied Buck, easing back again, feeling
relief that his visitor was not Brownell or some of
Brownell's riders. "Who's with you, Wyatt?"

Kilgore did not answer. He continued to study
Buck's battered chest and stomach, his blood-shot
eyes, and swollen lips. He turned, gave a sharp command, and stepped forth into the room as four other
men came along, too. Behind them, lingering in the
doorway, Milt stood and Mahalia lingered.

Kilgore jerked a thumb backward. "Who's your
friend?" he asked, meaning Milt.

"Feller I trailed with this past summer. Milton
Bond. He's from the Panhandle country." Buck's gaze
toward big Milt grew sardonic. "He eats like a horse,
rides like a Comanche, and fights like a herd of stal-
lions. Milt, this here is Wyatt Kilgore. He owns the
Fishhook outfit northeast of here."

Milt gravely nodded. He made no attempt to push
ahead and shake Kilgore's fist. Wyatt also nodded,
then in his brisk way he dismissed Milt, poked a
stubby thumb at the four solemn men standing close,
and said: "Johnny Gallatin, Forest Morgan, Pete
Slocum, an' Badger Clark." He spat those names out,

making no attempt to indicate by look or gesture which name went with which man. "These are four of my Fishhook riders. There's a fifth one . . . Sam Potter . . . the feller you belted this morning . . . he's not along on purpose. But these four are good men. They were with me before Brownell come. They can be trusted."

Kilgore was plainly in a hurry. No one interrupted him, but the strangers in that room kept switching their gazes, measuring and assessing one another, doing this covertly, very carefully. There was a slightly awkward atmosphere here. Buck could feel it, could almost reach out and touch it. Yet those Fishhook riders looked staunch to him. Each of them seemed to be solid, earthy, roughly honest, and roughly loyal. Typical range men.

"Listen to me, Buckley," snapped Wyatt Kilgore. He paused, twisted, and put a calculating look back at Milton Bond. "And you listen, too," he ordered. "That is . . . if you're with Buck in this. If you're not, you'd better go get your horse right now and pile up a heap of miles under him between now and sunset."

"Aw," grumbled big Milt in a discouraged voice. "I'm plumb tuckered from so much ridin' lately. I just sort of figured I'd hang and rattle around here for a spell. That is unless you west Texas boys commence beatin' on me. Then, of course, I'll have to leave because, you see, there's so much of me to hurt."

Kilgore's riders grinned over at Milt. He didn't grin back, but he solemnly winked. Kilgore faced forward again. He started to say something, checked himself, and began over. "When'll you be able to ride?" he asked. "And don't tell me right now, because this is no time for heroics. I need you, Buck, but not if you're goin' to fold up on me halfway through what's got to be done."

"Tonight maybe, Wyatt. Tomorrow that is for sure."

Over by the door Mahalia let her breath out in an audible sigh. Several of those rough, armed men looked quickly at her and quickly away. Kilgore was not one of them. He nodded at Buck, lying there on his bed. He was brusque and business-like.

"How about your friend? Will he ride, too?"

Buck, resenting Kilgore's brusqueness a little, said: "Ride where? What've you got on your mind, Wyatt?"

Kilgore tilted back his hat. He looked thoughtfully for a while, speculatively. "Well," he ultimately said, slowing his words down for the first time since entering the room, "it's been in the making for a long time, Buck, but you comin' back like this sort of threw a wrench into the gears." Kilgore fell silent again for a moment. He seemed to be carefully phrasing words this time. "Your pa and a couple of others . . . and me . . . we planned on bringing the Rangers in here. Brownell found out about it. Don't ask me how. None of us knows."

"How long ago was that?" Buck asked.

Kilgore gravely nodded. "I know what you're thinkin', and you're plumb right. He found out about it the day before your pa was killed."

Kilgore stopped speaking. He and Buck exchanged a long, long look. Buck murmured quietly: "I sort of thought that's how it happened, Wyatt. I had a lot of time to think on my ride back from Fishhook."

"And after you got back here . . . ?" asked Kilgore, his eyes darkening with hard irony. "What did you think then?"

"I knew, Wyatt. The second I saw those men waiting for me, I knew. It had to be either you or Justin. You hadn't had time to send a man to Tenawa, so it had to be Justin."

Kilgore's tough lips dropped. "That's about how it happened with us, too. I never talked to Justin Frazier. I never liked him, you'll recollect. But someone talked to him, someone had to, otherwise he wouldn't have known we were sendin' for the Texas Rangers."

"Pa," said Buck softly.

From back by the door Mahalia, who had been following this conversation closely, scarcely breathing, looking paler with the passing moments, spoke up: "Wyatt, I can't believe it. Not Justin Frazier."

Kilgore turned. He put those dark, ironic eyes of his on her. "It had to be, Mahalia. Brownell knew about our scheme and the next day Dave died."

Beside Mahalia, big Milt Bond said: "Something's troublin' me, Mister Kilgore. How come Brownell to single out Buck's pa and none of the others who were in on this thing?"

"I can only guess about that," answered the swarthy, wiry cattleman. "Frazier didn't know I was in it. Obviously Dave didn't name the others. Otherwise we'd be lyin' beside Dave right now."

Buck drew Kilgore's attention back around. "It's been quite a while since Pa was killed, Wyatt. What've you fellers been doin' since then?"

"Two more died after your pa got it. One was killed

in his yard like Dave, the other one was found dead seventeen miles east o' here. He'd been the one we'd decided should make the ride for the Rangers. Since then, Buck, we've done nothing. We've been waiting."

"For what?"

"You'll find out. Right now I can't hang around. If we're seen together, it won't take Brownell more'n a second or two to figure out we're up to something. Then . . . two more graves. What I want from you now, Buck, is a promise to meet me at Fishhook . . . ten o'clock tonight. You an' your friend . . . and your guns . . . with fresh horses and two canteens of water."

Milt spoke up again. "You're being kind of melo-dramatic, aren't you?"

It was the wrong thing to say to vinegary Wyatt Kilgore. "Listen, you," the piqued cowman said in a knife-edged voice. "If you want to ride on, get going. If you're fixin' to stay an' help, just keep your big mouth closed and your big ears open."

Milt sagged there in the doorway, looking steadily down into Kilgore's face. His expression did not change but his gaze was long and narrow and unblinking.

Buck broke it up between those two. "How many of us will there be?" he asked Kilgore.

"Enough. Anyway, that's my worry, not yours. All you've got to do is get over to my place without being seen on the way." Kilgore cocked his head, looking skeptically at Buckley. "And you'd better remember something, too . . . one word in the wrong place, even one hint, and there won't be any more male Baylors around."

Kilgore swung toward the door. He jerked his head

at those silent Fishhook riders. The five of them walked out through the parlor, and left the house. Buck and Milt Bond and Buck's mother heard them break away from the house in a hard run, heading northeast.

Milt sighed, looking steadily over at Buck. "For such a little feller he's sure hard to get along with."

It wasn't Buck who commented on this; it was Mahalia. "Buck's pa always put a lot of store by Wyatt Kilgore. They were never really close, not like Dave was with Justin Frazier, but I've heard him say it a hundred times . . . if he had to pick a man to stand with him in a fight, it'd be Wyatt Kilgore."

Buck took a big breath, held it, and let it slowly out. His ribs ached but the nausea that had lingered after his savage beating by Brownell's man was gone. "Ma, I could do with a bit of food," he said, and waited until his mother was gone to speak to Milt Bond.

"I thought I was alone in this. I'd about lost faith in the neighbors, Milt, after talkin' to Frazier last night."

Milt shoved off the door, ambled deeper into the room, and sat down. "Nice feller, this Justin Frazier," he dryly remarked. "But I reckon we can't blame him too much because you're a damned fool."

"What do you mean a damned fool, Milt? I've known that feller since I was a cub. All of us around here always thought real highly of Justin Frazier."

"Still," retorted Milt, "in a thing like this, pardner, no matter where it finds you . . . never tell anybody anything. Just do your snoopin' and, when you're sure which one is a louse and which one is not, start eliminatin' lice."

Buck snorted. "Hindsight's better'n foresight," he

said. "You'd have done the same thing I did, an' you know it."

Milt wouldn't admit this; he changed the subject. "Kilgore took a long chance comin' here," he mused. "Suppose those bully boys of Brownell's had still been here?"

"You'd have seen one hell of a massacre," stated Buck, and levered himself upright with his elbows. "Kilgore's a holy terror when he gets wound up. I remember one time when I was a kid he treed the town and locked the constable in his own jailhouse. It cost him a two-hundred-dollar fine, but he sure made history that night."

"Speakin' of constables," said Milt, still looking thoughtful, "is there one in Tenawa?"

Buck shrugged. "I just got back last night, remember. I haven't been to town yet."

Milt stroked his chin a moment, then stood up, got Buck's shirt, shook it once, and held it out. "Come on," he ordered. "You've had all the babyin' you're going to get. Put this on an' let's go out to the kitchen. I'm hungry enough to eat barbecued bear."

Buck got up, but it took him a long time to get into the shirt, and he had no real appetite after he was standing, either. His stomach felt like it was filled to the brim with some kind of corrosive acid.

He looked at himself in the mirror and turned away to follow Milt out of the little bedroom. He promised himself a return go-round with that green-eyed man who used doeskin gloves to keep from skinning his knuckles.

SIX

They were outside with the final red rays of a lowering sun painting their world with bold strokes when Milt sighted a rider and nudged Buck, raised an arm, and pointed.

"Can't be trouble . . . only one man," Milt said. "I've got this Brownell figured as a feller who uses force like a sledgehammer. Never send one man, send three."

Milt stood up off the bench at the barn where they were sitting, teetered there a second longer, studying the oncoming rider, then stepped across to the barn's front opening.

"Whoever it is, he isn't comin' to see me, so I'll just sort of stand back in here, and, when the fur begins to fly, I'll just sort of step out again."

Buck said nothing, but after Milt had disappeared, he arose, watched the slowly oncoming rider for a moment, went over to a trough, and sluiced cool water over his battered face, crushed his hat back on, and returned to the bench. He was sitting casually in barn shade when Milt hissed at him from within the barn.

"It's a girl, Buck. Now, what the hell?"

It was, indeed, a girl. Buck hadn't been watching the last few minutes. He didn't want to give the impression that he was uneasy or interested. Now, though, he looked outward. Recognition came slowly. Although he'd practically grown up with Kathleen Frazier, he'd been gone nearly a year. He saw now that this one year had been a crucial one in the life of Justin Frazier's gangling, tomboy daughter. When he'd ridden away, she'd been half girl, half woman, with the budding promise of womanhood visible, but with an awkwardness, a self-conscious resentment of it making her moody and difficult and sometimes downright antagonistic. He'd remembered her like this those few times he'd remembered her at all.

This, though, he saw, was not the same Kathy at all. She was still long-limbed. She still had girlhood's little sprinkle of freckles across the saddle of her nose. Her skin was still creamy and her eyes still very faintly lifted at their outer edges. But otherwise the gangling girl was completely gone. She was still a hundred yards out, looking solemnly ahead where Buck sat, when from within the barn came a long, low moan of masculine appreciation.

Buck tossed aside the cured blade of grass he'd been toying with. He stood up. She rode across the yard toward him without taking her eyes off his face for a second. She had the blackest hair imaginable; her mouth was wide and gentle and heavy, with a shapeliness that struck down into Buck. She wore a buckskin-colored riding blouse, full with the roundness of her upper body, and her split riding skirt was shades darker, a sort of sorrel color. She halted ten feet away and made a little-girl, tentative smile downward.

"Hello, Buck," she said, and waited.

"Hello, Kathy."

He stepped over to put a hand lightly upon the reins, and she swung down, came along the side of her animal into barn shade near him, and acted neither awkward nor moody.

He dropped the reins. "You've changed," he said, forgetting to ask her to sit. "You've grown up, Kathy."

Her smile warmed a little. "It's been almost a year. And before that for another year I didn't see much of you."

He understood. He'd loped over to the Hardesty place every chance he'd had those two previous years. He'd not forgotten her, but she was the kid he'd grown up with, the person he'd taken for granted, and Carol . . . that had been altogether different.

She went past to the bench, stood looking at it, then turned and sat down. "You've changed, too. You didn't used to go around getting into fights."

He raised his eyebrows at her.

"Your face. Don't tell me you did that falling off a horse."

He thought of something sharp to say but didn't say it. He smiled at her. "A pigeon kicked me," he said, walked over and stopped in front of her, still smiling. "Kathy, this takes a little gettin' used to. You growin' up on me like this."

A little faint color surged into her face. She looked away and back again. "Pa told me you rode over last night. It was pretty late, though, and we were asleep. I came over today to repay your-call."

So Justin had said his midnight visit was simply a social call, had he? Buck dropped his head. He was not a man who could hide his feelings without doing it behind a wide hat brim.

"We heard you'd been killed at Dodge City, Buck."

"I heard that, too," he replied, lifting his head, making that little crinkly smile again. "But I never really believed it, Kathy." He stepped over and sat down beside her. "Tell me about things this past year."

She was profiled to him. Where evening shadows touched across her, there was a wholesome kind of beauty. He saw the lift and drop of her breasts as she breathed, and the soft turning of her throat, the flawlessness of her complexion and the steady, dreamy outward run of her gaze.

"There's not a lot to tell. Pa said you knew about your father." She swung, searching his face. "I cried for you, Buckley, because you were gone and didn't know. That's not the only reason, though."

"The other reason, Kathy?"

"We grew up together, remember? I knew you better than . . . almost anyone else. I knew your temper, Buck. You'd come back and find out how he died and you'd go after his murderers. You could be killed."

Buck stooped, plucked another blade of grass, popped it between his teeth, and gently chewed. What did she really know? He recalled her as an observant person. Even as a tomboy girl, racing over the countryside on some half-broken horse, she'd been shrewd and thoughtful and wise—wise beyond her years, he thought now. He chewed and looked out into the settling late afternoon and said: "Kathy, tell me about Cleve Brownell."

She was silent a long time, coming to a decision. She shook her head at him. "Not your first day home, Buck. Not the first time we've seen each other after so long." She paused, drew in a breath, changed her tone, and said: "Do you remember my little Ginger mare? Well, she had a colt this spring. And Pa's old War Bonnet stud horse . . . he died last winter. Pa said as near as he could reckon it, War Bonnet was twenty-eight years old. He rode him in the war."

Her voice ran softly on resurrecting memories for him, working its soothing magic, while around them shadows puddled and thickened and became the carpet of the evening.

He spat out the blade of dried grass. "You make this past year seem a lifetime, Kathy."

Her tone turned grave. "In a lot of ways it's been a lifetime."

"Yeah," he dryly murmured, "it sure has." He cast an eye skyward, closely estimated the time, and stood up, twisted, and gazed down at her. "I can't get over how you've changed in one year."

She arose, accepting his hint that she should go now. "Two years, really," she said, looking up into his eyes.

He nodded, understanding what she meant by this, feeling the return of pain at this innuendo. Her gaze darkened toward him, sharing some of his anguish.

"Maybe . . . ," she murmured, "maybe, when you get a little time, we could go riding some evening like we used to, Buck."

He made no answer. He caught the reins of her horse, swept them up, and held the horse, waiting for her to mount. This was for him a troubled moment of bittersweet recollections of their childhood together. It brought a crowding host of sad memories flooding over him.

She mounted, took up the reins, and sat a moment, looking downward. "Be careful," she said. "Be careful and tell your mother hello for me."

He stepped back and watched her rein around and ride out of the yard. He lost her in the outward darkness but did not turn back to the bench until the last echo of her passage died out entirely to the northwest.

Milt came forth from the barn. He cast a sidelong look at Buck on the bench, shuffled his feet, and leaned there on the barn's front wall, saying nothing at all, which was not like Milt who always had some observation to offer.

Time ran on, evening faded into night. Corralled horses blew their noses and gradually those little pinpricks of light became noticeable in the high vault of heaven.

Mahalia came out, up at the house, called down the yard that supper was ready, and Buck got up, struck at nonexistent dust on his trouser legs, said—"Come on."—to Milt, and they went trooping toward the ranch house side-by-side, two tall, angular, heavy-boned men, each occupied with his private thoughts.

Near the verandah Milt said: "I forked feed to the horses." He said this to fetch Buck back to the present. "Never liked to ride a horse on a full belly or an empty one."

99

Buck halted, turned, and said: "Don't mention her riding over here in front of Ma."

Milt said: "Sure not."

They went inside, passed through to the kitchen and beyond to the little rear porch where the roller towel, the lye soap, and the wash basin stood, cleansed themselves, and came to the table. Mahalia brought the food, poured coffee, sat down, lowered her gray head, and asked the Lord to bless the board, then looked first at her son, then at his friend, and said to Buckley: "She's become a woman, hasn't she, Son?"

Milt took up his cup and drank deeply of the coffee. Over its rim he looked straight over at Buck.

"She's grown up, all right," agreed Buck, and went to work on his fried meat as though this closed the subject.

"I haven't seen her in a long time," said Mahalia, faintly frowning down at her own plate, making no move to eat. "When you two were little, she was like a daughter."

"Ma, pass the potatoes, will you?"

"Buckley . . . she wouldn't know."

Milt said to Mahalia, seeing the danger signals in Buck's face and knowing them for what they were—you couldn't share a hundred campfires with a man and not know him this well: "Funny how home cookin' brings back memories to a feller, ma'am. Now, you take these here potatoes, an' that there gravy. When I was a button, my granny used to flavor 'em the same way, an' never since have I ever tasted 'em just like that, until tonight. Tell me . . . is it the pepper or the sage that gives 'em that taste?"

Mahalia's eyes swung. She considered big Milt Bond steadily for a silent moment, then she acquiesced, letting him change the subject. But when she answered him, her voice had none of the lilt a woman's voice ordinarily possesses when her food is praised.

"I guess, more than anything else, it's just doing something over and over until you get all the measurements down in your head, Mister Bond."

"Milt, ma'am. Just plain Milt. Well, they sure are good. That's the one thing I believe a feller misses most on trail drives . . . real cookin'."

Nothing more was said until, near the end of the meal, Mahalia looked at them both. "Be careful tonight. Be very careful. I know Wyatt is a clever man, boys. I also know Cleve Brownell is just as clever."

That was all she told them before they left the house, but it would have been abundantly clear to anyone who only casually looked into her face that Mahalia Baylor was full of apprehension and misgivings and anxiety.

They saddled up with the night's solid formlessness out over the land in all directions. They rode out, heading northeast, saying very little, each busy with his own thoughts, their horses fresh, their booted carbines loaded, and their saddle canteens lashed flat so they would make no noise at all.

As they passed beyond sight of the solitary lamp glow from the Baylor Ranch, Milt said: "What'll Kilgore have in mind, you reckon?"

"Damned if I know," answered Buck. "But I'll tell you this much. It'll be trouble for somebody."

SEVEN

Wyatt Kilgore's ranch had lights in three places: the main house, the bunkhouse, and the barn. From a mile out Buck and Milt saw this three-fold brightness and set their course by it. The moon was near to rising but it would only be a little fuller than it had been the night before, so it would shed a bare minimum of its cold, impersonal milky light, and otherwise this would be a dark night.

When they came down into the Fishhook yard, two men stepped forth to halt them. One was a rider who had accompanied Kilgore to the Baylor place earlier this same day; the other man was a rancher from east of Tenawa who Buck knew only distantly, yet who he now recognized and who also recognized him. Wyatt Kilgore's man jerked his head wordlessly. He and his companion faded out into the surrounding darkness again, to resume their sentinel positions.

Milt leaned across to say quietly: "Looks like they've got a small army here. You reckon Kilgore's aimin' to brace the town?"

Buck shrugged, rode across to the barn area where several men were standing, and swung down. Kilgore stepped clear of the dark shapes over there and swung forward. He nodded to Buck, to Milt, shot a quick look at their horses, their canteens and carbine boots, then said: "All right. The others'll be ready to ride in a few minutes. You two stand easy." He turned away. Buck halted him with words.

"What's this all about?"

"You'll find out," snapped Kilgore, obviously tense and anxious.

"Sure we will," said Buck in the same sharp way. "But we want to know now, not later."

Kilgore twisted, put a stony look at Buck, and said: "No one else has questioned me, Buckley. The fewer people who know, the better our chances of success."

Buck stood easy, reins in one hand, head a little to one side. "I got hell whaled out of me today, remember? My pa was killed by Brownell. I reckon you can tell me, Wyatt."

Kilgore's testy gaze flashed. He was silent for a moment. "Brownell's sent four of his men south to the border," he finally explained. "Other times, when he's done that, his men return with a drove of Mex beef."

"How do you know he's done that?"

Kilgore's thin lips drew downward. "Brownell's not the only one who uses spies, Buck. I learned how to do that after he planted Sam Potter in my bunkhouse. Only I use bartenders and livery swampers an' store clerks in town. That answer you?"

"Partly," replied Buck. "What's your plan?"

Kilgore shrugged. "Nothing very complicated. Just

go after those four men. Take 'em before they get the cattle or after . . . it doesn't make much difference . . . but take 'em." Kilgore's jaw snapped closed. He looked at those two big men a moment longer, then swung back toward the barn where men were emerging, leading horses.

Milt watched him go with a grave expression. "He's got the right idea, but the wrong way o' doing it," he muttered. He might have said more but at this juncture those two sentinels from across the yard came along in a trot. Buck swung, stepped over, and halted them.

"What is it?" he demanded.

"Riders," said Kilgore's man a little breathlessly. "Riders out in the night. We heard 'em."

Buck was unimpressed. "More fellers comin' in," he suggested.

Kilgore's cowboy emphatically shook his head. "Nope. Everybody's here. I know. That's been my job."

Buck left Milt with their horses and hastened over where a number of grim-visaged armed cowmen were in conversation with Wyatt Kilgore. Before the sentries could interrupt, Buck shouldered in among those stalwart shapes and sounded the warning. In conclusion, he said to Wyatt: "What made you think, if Brownell planted a man in your bunkhouse, he didn't do the same thing at the other ranches?"

"I know he did," shot back Kilgore, holding a carbine in the crook of his arm. "But us cowmen knew them, and every man here's taken steps. . . ."

"Somebody didn't," interrupted Buck. "Somebody blundered." He turned, called out to the men at the barn: "Kill that damned light!" He caught the cowboy

GET
4 FREE BOOKS!

You can have the best Westerns delivered to your door for less than what you'd pay in a bookstore or online. Sign up for one of our book clubs today, and we'll send you 4 FREE* BOOKS, worth $23.96, just for trying it out...with no obligation to buy, ever!

———◆◆◆———

Authors include classic writers such as
LOUIS L'AMOUR, MAX BRAND, ZANE GREY
and more; PLUS new authors such as
COTTON SMITH, TIM CHAMPLIN, JOHNNY D. BOGGS
and others.

———◆◆◆———

As a book club member you also receive the following special benefits:
- **30% OFF all orders through our website & telecenter!**
- **Exclusive access to special discounts!**
- **Convenient home delivery and 10 days to return any books you don't want to keep.**

There is no minimum number of books to buy,
and you may cancel membership at any time.
See back to sign up!

*Please include $2.00 for shipping and handling.

YES! ☐

Sign me up for the Leisure Western Book Club and send my FOUR FREE BOOKS! If I choose to stay in the club, I will pay only $13.44* each month, a savings of $10.52!

NAME: _____

ADDRESS: _____

_____

TELEPHONE: _____

E-MAIL: _____

☐ **I WANT TO PAY BY CREDIT CARD.**

☐ VISA ☐ MasterCard ☐ DISCOVER

ACCOUNT #: _____

EXPIRATION DATE: _____

SIGNATURE: _____

Send this card along with $2.00 shipping & handling to:

**Leisure Western Book Club
20 Academy Street
Norwalk, CT 06850-4032**

Or fax (must include credit card information!) to: 610.995.9274.
You can also sign up online at www.dorchesterpub.com.

*Plus $2.00 for shipping. Offer open to residents of the U.S. and Canada only.
Canadian residents please call 1.800.481.9191 for pricing information.
If under 18, a parent or guardian must sign. Terms, prices and conditions subject to change. Subscription subject
to acceptance. Dorchester Publishing reserves the right to reject any order or cancel any subscription.

JOIN NOW!

sentry by the arm and pointed toward the main house and the bunkhouse. "Kill those lights, too."

The armed men in the yard, sensing trouble, began drifting over where Kilgore, Buck, and the others stood. There were, Buck thought, close to twenty of them. Some he recognized, some he did not. He considered it very likely that among this crowd was at least one Brownell man. This was not the time, however, to try and find him. He took Wyatt Kilgore by the arm, led him off a goodly distance, and said: "Who else knows besides Milt and me what you planned to do?"

Kilgore shook his head. "Only Farraday of the Trinity Ranch. You remember him, don't you?"

Buck remembered Steve Farraday. He owned the Trinity outfit six miles south of Tenawa. He was a gruff older man whose range ran down along the border. Farraday was somewhat of a legend in the Tenawa country. He'd fought more Mexican marauders than anyone else because his ranch was the first outfit raiders hit after crossing the river out of Mexico. He hired only the toughest riders and rumor had it he didn't hire men because they were good cowboys, but because they were experienced gunmen. Farraday, Buck now thought, was the last man among all those gathered in Kilgore's yard who would be likely to tip off Brownell.

"You sure none of the others know?" he asked.

Kilgore was certain, but he was also impatient. "We can't stand around here talkin'," he snarled. "We got to find out who those riders are out there in the dark."

Buck said swiftly: "Do nothing. Go back, tell everyone to take their horses and ride out of here. Tell 'em to go on home."

"What?"

"Listen, Wyatt, those riders out there can only belong to one man. He's got wind of something goin' on out here tonight. Unless you're ready to fight him here and now, you'd better tell everyone to beat it for home. Tell them you called them together to plan a big roundup. Brownell'll go after them, askin' questions. If they only know what you tell 'em now, that's all they'll be able to tell Brownell. Now, get moving. It's up to you. Fight now, or put it off until we're better prepared."

"How?" Kilgore demanded. "How, better prepared?"

Buck's patience was slipping in the face of the older man's stubbornness and density. "You damned fool," he snarled at Kilgore. "Brownell would have known by dawn all of us were gone. How long do you think it'd take him to smell bad trouble . . . us leavin' right after his own men left? Kilgore, he'd round up every hostage in the country, an' from what I've learnt this far about him, he'll kill some of 'em."

When Buck stopped speaking, Kilgore said: "He's not going to believe this . . . about us all meetin' here tonight to plan a big roundup."

"If you can think of something better, then do it," directed Buck. "But until then rely on the fact that he will have doubts, not strong ones perhaps, but strong enough to hold off startin' anything for a day or two, I hope."

Kilgore stood there, glaring, his face twisted into an ugly expression. He had a difficult decision to make and there was a knot in his belly as large as a man's fist. He turned abruptly and strode back toward the barn where that dark, milling crowd of armed men stood.

Buck watched him go. He did not know which way Kilgore would decide, to fight or break it up, but in either case he wished to be near Milt and his saddle animal, so he hiked out through the dust and the gloom, found Milt where he'd left him, and related what had taken place.

Milt had an idea. "Let's get out of here, Buck. Let's slip 'way out around Brownell's town and head for the border ourselves. Leave these fellers to sweat this out their own way. From tonight on, Brownell's goin' to be watchin' these fellers like a hawk. Particularly Kilgore. He'll be too busy to worry much about you an' me, and, even if we can't dry-gulch his rustler team, we sure as hell can get out of the country, find a Ranger post, an' fetch back help."

Buck stood expressionlessly watching that dark area over by the barn where Kilgore was swiftly speaking to the assembled ranchers and their cowboys. He'd heard Milt's suggestion. It sounded feasible to him. He started to turn, to speak to Milt, when a man glided up to them from behind, identified himself as a watcher Kilgore had detailed out on the southern range, and said: "Brownell's comin' in. He's got six of his toughest gunfighters with him." This man then glided on forward toward the men at the barn, who were breaking up, some mounting their horses, some walking off, leading their animals, but all of them going in diverse directions.

Buck let out a pent-up breath. "He's sending them home. He's not going to make a fight of it." He reached for his reins, jerked his head at Milt, and the pair of them began walking on across the yard toward Kilgore's dark, low, and fort-like adobe residence. They got over there without interruption, turned to see the nearly empty yard, and also see dim shapes of mounted men begin to filter into the yard from various directions. These riders came quietly, converging upon Wyatt Kilgore and rough old Steve Farraday by the barn. They did not speak or dismount as they halted, surrounding Kilgore and Farraday. They simply sat there, looking down.

Milt whispered: "I wouldn't be in Kilgore's boots right now for a farm in Iowa. Those are killers, every last one of 'em."

Buck hissed for silence. A man in a white shirt was approaching from the roadway entrance to the Fishhook yard. Neither Milt nor Buck could see this man's face clearly because of distance and the poor light, but they had no doubts about this stranger's identity.

"Brownell," whispered Buck.

Milt nodded.

They studied Cleve Brownell closely, each with a lethal reason for this. They wanted to be able to recognize the outlaw leader when they met again. Across the intervening distance they heard Brownell speak, as he halted, joined that circle of riders around Kilgore and Farraday, and sat there like stone, looking downward.

"Heard you were havin' some kind of a meetin' out here tonight, Kilgore. Thought I'd ride out and listen in. Sorry I was late, but you wouldn't mind tellin' me what it was all about, would you?"

Brownell's voice was quietly deadly, but it was not

an unpleasant or rough voice. Buck clenched his fists, thinking it had been this man's voice which had captivated Carol Hardesty, his smooth way of saying things and the softness of his tone.

Kilgore's answer was gruff. "Any law against cowmen gettin' together to plan a roundup? We been doing this for ten years, Brownell."

"No," came that resonant, rich voice. "No, no law against that . . . if that's what you were doing."

"Ask Farraday here," retorted Kilgore. "Ask any of the others. You must've seen 'em leavin'."

Brownell was silent for a time. He looked out over Fishhook's empty yard. His gaze lingered longest over where Kilgore's riders were standing in a little group at the bunkhouse. He said: "I see only four of your riders, Kilgore. Where is the fifth man?"

Buck held his breath. He had until this moment completely forgotten Brownell's spy, Sam Potter, the man he had knocked senseless.

"He's over at my line shack," came back Kilgore's solid answer to this. "I sent him over there to clean a water hole and look around for some first-calf heifers we haven't seen in a week or so. Anything wrong with that?"

Brownell swung his attention back. He said: "What're you so touchy about, Kilgore? I'm only asking a few questions."

Kilgore relaxed. Buck and Milt saw some of the rigidity leave him. When Kilgore answered, his voice sounded less brittle, less antagonistic. "How am I supposed to feel, standin' here in my own yard with six of your riders surroundin' me?"

Brownell's even teeth flashed whitely in the gloom. "A little scairt," the outlaw chieftain said candidly. "You're supposed to feel a little scairt, Kilgore. I hope you do . . . because if you don't . . . if you're tryin' to work up something against me. . ." Brownell let his voice trail off into significant silence. He kept right on smiling down at the two surrounded men before the barn. "You got a nice ranch here, Kilgore . . . you, too, Farraday . . . be a real shame if the pair of you had to bow out an' leave everything to your next of kin."

Brownell shortened his reins. He shot a look at his mounted riders. He made a scarcely noticeable movement with his head. The gunfighters began moving, began edging their mounts around away from Kilgore and Farraday. As his men walked their horses away, back toward the roadway entrance to Fishhook's yard, Cleve Brownell leaned down a little.

"After this, hold your cattlemen's meetings in broad daylight," he ordered. "And let me know when you're holdin' 'em. I want to sit in." He paused a moment, looking from Kilgore to Farraday. "Whatever you might have in the backs of your minds, boys . . . don't try it. If you do, there'll be enough dead men in the Tenawa country to stack like cordwood . . . and not only dead *men*."

Brownell straightened up, spun his horse, and rode off after his gunfighters.

EIGHT

Buck and Milt Bond left Wyatt Kilgore's place, riding south through a night made soft, made ghostly, by the sickle moon. For a long while neither of them spoke. Because they were passing along the same route Brownell had taken back toward Tenawa with his outlaws, they were concerned less with conversation than they were with listening.

After a while, with Tenawa's lights showing dead ahead, Buck eased off easterly to pass far out around the town. He thought, as Milt also thought, that Brownell and his riders would head straight for Tenawa. They spoke a little back and forth, discussing the happenings of this night, presenting their separate views and summaries and scarcely heeded the stillness until, with the lights of Frank Hardesty's place on their left, a pair of riders suddenly loomed up silently cutting diagonally across their route, evidently returning to Tenawa from some place far out.

Fortunately these two unidentified riders did not see Buck and Milt until they had themselves been seen, then it was too late. Although both men instantly dropped their right hands, Milt sang out harshly and wig-wagged his already palmed six-gun.

"Don't do it, boys! You're a dollar short and an hour late."

The strangers drew rein. They were some eighty feet away. Buck, cautious but not greatly concerned, thought it likely that these were cowhands from some outlying ranch. Then one of those men ground out a hard curse and Buck's head snapped erect. That voice was the same one he'd heard earlier when a green-eyed, lantern-jawed man had drawn a pair of doeskin roping gloves over big knuckles, then beat him sense-less while two other of Brownell's men had held him.

Buck sat there, turning cold and icily speculative. He had not recognized this man back at the Kilgore place and yet he thought the green-eyed man had to have been there. But if that were so—what was he do-ing this far out of town now?

"What's your name?" he called forward. "You . . . the feller who just cussed . . . what's your name?"

"None of your damned business," shot back Brownell's hired gunman.

Milt cocked his six-gun. That sharp, little, jarring sound carried across the distance handily and an an-swer came back almost breathlessly to Buck's query.

"Tom Thorne."

Milt leaned far over, dropped his voice low, and murmured: "We're in luck. I recognize that feller. He's the one who overhauled your riggin' back at your ma's place."

Buck looked at the other man, thought he recognized his smaller size, his tilted-back hat, and his easy manner as belonging to the gunman who had talked to him in his own barn, who had tossed Buck's six-gun into the empty manger.

Milt suddenly said: "Get down."

Brownell's men dismounted.

"Drop your guns and step away from those saddle boots."

This time obedience was slower and the smaller of those two rustlers seemed to be balancing forward on the balls of his feet as though to whip around behind his horse.

Buck spoke to the smaller man, leveling his gun and cocking it, leaning forward in the saddle as he spoke. "You go ahead and jump, mister, and I'll promise you one thing. Brownell will have two to bury before sunup."

The small man didn't jump. He took three steps clear of his horse and muttered a warning to his companion. Thorne also stepped clear.

"The guns," Milt prompted, looping his reins and kicking his right leg free. "Drop 'em or use 'em. I don't give a damn which."

Both outlaws let their guns fall. Tom Thorne said bitterly: "You damned fools will regret this." It was obvious he had no idea yet who his antagonists were.

Buck and Milt swung down. They led their horses sixty feet straight ahead, then halted. Now Thorne and his friend got a good long look and both of them turned stiff with astonishment.

Milt carefully holstered his six-gun, unbuckled his shell belt, handed it along with his reins and his hat to

113

Buck, and broadly, lazily smiled. "I got to prove to you I can hit harder than he can," he told Buck. "You just watch how this is done." He faced Thorne, squared himself around, and went forward. The smaller gunman's expression became wire-tight. He was not smiling at all now.

Thorne's eyes squeezed together. He shuffled his feet a little and brought up his hands. Milt balked at this and said: "Better put on those fancy little gloves, feller. I'd sure hate to see you bruise your hands." He waited, but Tom Thorne made no move to reach for his gloves. He put his whole attention upon Milt, watching every move Milt made, then, when Milt stood there making no additional move forward, but stood measuring his enemy, Thorne said over Milt's shoulder to Buck: "You're a bigger fool than I thought, Baylor. You figure this gettin' even will end here?"

Milt was moving when Buck put up his gun and stepped forward saying: "Say it in plain words, Thorne. What did you mean by that remark?"

Milt gave Thorne time to answer before going after him. The gunman said: "The two of you goin' up against Brownell . . . hell, you don't stand the chance of a lame duck in a nest of coyotes. But even if you did, Baylor, you're overlookin' something. Even if you got away with it . . . there'd still be your ma and the others hereabouts."

Milt called Thorne a name and danced forward. "I figured," he said, bobbing and weaving close to the gunman, "you were the kind that fights women and men with their arms twisted behind 'em. I figured that this mornin' at the Baylor place."

Thorne edged away from big Milt. He stepped left, then stepped right. He was no novice at this game. He said no more and neither did Milt nor Buck.

Thorne dropped down, ran a flicking jab under Milt's guard that glanced off a belt buckle. He jumped clear as a whistling blow sang close, spun away, and grinned at Milt.

"You clumsy ox," he said. "You big dumb clumsy ox."

Milt's teeth shone in a bleak grin. He made no comment on this. He only pushed on, pressing Thorne, crowding him, keeping him moving backward and maneuvering him toward his own saddle horse. Thorne stopped, sprang ahead, and threw a fast right hand that skidded along Milt's guarding forearm. This time he did not get away quickly enough. Milt's maul-like fist lashed out, struck with the sound of a faraway pistol shot against Thorne's jaw, and Brownell's gunman staggered.

Over his shoulder to Buck, Milt called: "An' that was just the light one, the easy one!"

They circled one another, crouched and pawing, moving carefully until Thorne dropped down to shoot another fist under Milt's guard as he'd done before. But Milt knew this trick now. He stepped back, let Thorne's fist slash emptiness, stepped in, and swung a looping blow that caught the green-eyed man flush in the belly. This blow made a meaty sound. Thorne's breath burst out. He straightened out of his crouch and stumbled away.

"Finish him!" exclaimed Buck.

Milt dropped his fists, shook his head, and said:

"Naw. He took five minutes on you this morning. I don't like to cheat a man, an' I figure, with interest an' all, he's got about ten minutes' worth of beatin' comin' back."

Thorne kept back-pedaling until twenty feet lay between them. He looked over where two six-guns lay in darkness gently shining. Milt, seeing that look, shook his head. "You'd never make it," he said. "Never in God's green world." He started for Thorne.

The smaller gunman, standing alone and off to one side, called encouragement to Thorne. He was living this fight. When a blow was thrown, he recoiled or rolled with it. When either combatant moved, he shifted his footing, too. In contrast, Buck Baylor stood like stone, only his eyes moving.

Milt caught a stinging blow along the side of the face and turned his head with it. He jumped in then, jumped out, feinting Thorne into a wild strike that missed. He made a lunge, took two hard blows along the left side, squared around, and hit Thorne three times in the middle, pawed him off, dropped down his right shoulder and held his right fist cocked. But Thorne got away, dropped hands, and sucked at the night air. Milt started stalking him, moving slowly, inexorably. He was grinning like a death's head.

They backed around, Milt pushing, Thorne retreating. When the pair of them passed close, Buck got a look at the green-eyed man's face. Thorne was sick. He'd been struck too many times in the stomach. He was sick and tiring.

Milt rushed him, lunging ahead with his right fist still cocked. Thorne jumped, caromed into the shoulder of his own saddle animal, bounced off, and caught that fired right fist flush in the mouth. Blood spewed; Thorne's knees sprung outward. He staggered ahead five feet past Milt. Buck could see his glazing stare and his broken mouth. He also saw Milt drop down flat, walk after Thorne, tap him lightly to bring him back around—and hit him so hard his fist was entirely lost in Thorne's middle.

As Tom Thorne went down all in a heap, his companion let off a great sigh and staggered. Milt turned, surveyed the smaller man, deliberately turned his back, and looked over at Buck.

"Satisfied?" he called. "Satisfied I can hit harder than he can?"

Buck didn't reply. Thorne was breathing with difficulty. Buck went across, rolled him over face down so he would not choke on his own blood, then looked gravely at Milt.

"We can't leave 'em here, Milt. You heard him. As soon as they're able, they'll go hunt up Brownell. There'll be retaliation for this, not against us but against the others, my ma an' Kilgore an' Farraday an' the others around Tenawa."

Milt blew on his knuckles, flexed his right hand, and seemed entirely preoccupied with this, as well he might be for that was his gun hand, too. Finally he beckoned the shorter gunman over and gazed fixedly at him while considering their predicament.

"We could shoot 'em," he suggested, saw Buck's frown over this, and added: "We could leave 'em tied up in somebody's barn around here somewhere." Then he shook his head over his own proposal. "Naw, they

117

might get loose. The only thing, then, is either shoot 'em or take 'em along."

They took them along. Thorne was tied in the saddle with his own lariat and the smaller gunman was detailed to supporting him. Milt rode beside the smaller man and Buck rode on the opposite side of Thorne. As they passed the Hardesty Ranch, Buck said to the smaller man: "What were you two doin' out here? How come you didn't head straight for town with the others?"

"There's a big bay horse at Hardesty's," came his reply. "Tom's been wantin' that critter, so we just split off an' went over to Hardesty's to get it."

"Why didn't you get it, then?"

"The old fool'd turned his horses out, the big bay along with the others."

Buck kept looking at the smaller man, his gaze deadly. "Haven't you done enough to Frank Hardesty?" he asked softly.

There was no reply to this. The smaller man read death in Baylor's face as clearly as though it had been broad daylight. He did not open his mouth.

Milt, also seeing the look in Buck's eyes, swung his head, looked out, then looked back. "Where are the men Brownell sent south?" he asked, getting away from the other topic. "Where will they meet the Mex cattle and what route will they follow?"

The smaller gunman shifted in his saddle. He made out that he was too occupied supporting Tom Thorne to answer. Big Milt reached over, caught him by the shoulder, and bore down cruelly with his vise-like fingers.

"South," gasped the gunfighter. "They go due south an' meet the herd near a place called Red Rock."

Milt let go. "You know the place?" he asked Buck.
"Yeah, I know it."

Buck rode for a full mile without speaking again or looking at the others. It took that long for the ferocity within him to dwindle, to ease off in his mind so that he could think of what lay ahead.

"Red Rock's a boulder field a little west of the way we're going now, Milt. The boundary line runs across it. There's a spring down there . . . about the only water anywhere around where you could hold a herd of beef. It's a place where Mex raiders used to rendezvous on their way back over the line after playing hell up in Texas." Buck looked over at the gunman. "Shake him," he said harshly. "Shake Thorne. He wasn't hit *that* hard."

The gunman obeyed. He shook Thorne's limp body. He grunted from the effort as the sagging killer listed far out of his saddle. He squeaked at Buck: "Help me . . . he's goin' to fall."

Buck reined closer, reached over, and caught Thorne's shirt. The sagging man's head aimlessly rolled and Buck, feeling a sudden premonition, dragged Thorne over toward him, pushed his face close, and stared. He suddenly reined up, halting Thorne's animal beside him, bent still closer and stared, then raised up looking over at Milt.

"He's dead."

Milt looked nonplussed. The smaller gunman drew up in his saddle, staring.

"His neck's broken," said Buck.

NINE

They stopped long enough to make a cairn and bury
Brownell's lieutenant. They flung his saddle atop the
mound along with his hat. Throughout all this the
smaller gunman was silent and apprehensive. When it
was all over, Thorne's horse had been turned loose and
the others were ready to go on. The gunman looked
across Thorne's grave and spoke to Buck.

"That's the man who killed your pa," he said,
stepped up over leather, and looked balefully downward. "I was there. I know."

"What else do you know?" Buck asked quietly.

"Not a whole lot more, just that your pa and some
others was plannin' trouble for Brownell. He heard
about it and sent some of us out to your pa's place."

"Go on."

"We rode into the yard. Your pa was repairin' a
buggy seat. He stood up. He didn't say nothin', but he
looked hard. Thorne drew his pistol, said . . . 'Compli-
ments o' Cleve Brownell' . . . and fired. Your pa fell
down, an', as we were lopin' out o' the yard, your ma

come scootin' out of the chicken house. I looked back an' seen her. So did Thorne, but she didn't do nothin' but run over where your pa lay an' we kept on ridin'."

Milt and Buck exchanged a look. Everything the gunman had related tallied perfectly with what Buck's mother had already told them.

Buck lifted his reins. "Let's go," he mumbled.

They rode along southward through star-washed hush without speaking again for a long while. It was Milt, piecing all this together in his mind, who eventually broke the silence among them.

"Tell me," he said to the gunman, "exactly how does this business of Brownell's work?"

"Well, we used to operate in Mexico. We turned a lot of beef down there. The trouble was the Mexes don't have any real good markets or much cash, either. Cleve said we were ridin' too hard for the money we made out of it, so we made a deal with some other fellers down there to rustle the cattle an' deliver 'em to us at the line. Then we'd trail 'em north, give 'em to some drover who was makin' up a drive, either on shares or on consignment, then we'd wait until he took 'em north, sold 'em, and brought us the money."

"Kind of risky, wasn't it?" asked Milt. "How'd you know you'd get your money?"

The gunman made a little crooked smile over at Milt. "Cleve always sent at least one o' us along with the drive. We got the money, all right. We only consigned the herds to honest men. Never had no trouble that way."

Buck said: "Why Tenawa? Why not some other town?"

The outlaw's shoulders rose and fell. "Cleve made the choice. He scouted a lot of border-country towns. He said Tenawa would do fine because it didn't have a Ranger post an' because most of the time the range men thereabouts was gone north on the drives. So, we moved in."

"We used to have a constable," said Buck. "He was an old feller named. . ."

"Yeah, I know. Well, he got it."

That was all the gunman would say concerning the killing of Tenawa's town constable. He shortly fell silent, but before he did, he verified what Kilgore had already said, that Cleve Brownell put some of his riders in the various bunkhouses as spies and that he'd had nearly a half dozen resisting townsmen and ranchers killed.

"It cowed the countryside."

"Yeah," said Buck, "but he had to have help. Someone around Tenawa had to work with him."

The gunman looked up, then down again. He was silent.

Milt raised his arm.

Buck shook his head at Milt. "Forget it," he commanded. "We know who it was, anyway."

For another mile or two they trudged along in silence. The southward country was desert. There was nopal and catclaw and yucca. There was also scrub sage and Spanish bayonet and, closer to the international line, boulders, whole fields of boulders. They started small and kept getting larger. They ranged in color from fish-belly gray to a kind of rusty-iron shade of bloody red. It was this last color that prompted Milt to say: "How much farther?"

"Two miles," answered Buck. "No more'n that."

Their prisoner began to get nervous the closer they got to the rendezvous site. He kept swinging his head, running his gaze here and there. Buck, seeing this, said: "Where do they meet? I don't hear any bawling cattle."

"You wouldn't hear 'em. They're dry as dirt by the time they get up here, an' footsore. You know where that spring is in the little grassy park among them boulders?"

"Yeah. Is that the place?"

"It is." The gunman slouched along for another thousand yards, arguing with himself, then he said grudgingly. "They put out sentries. If I didn't tell you this, I might get killed, too."

"You sure might," agreed big Milt, thumbed back his hat, and started onward where some dark and rocky upthrusts were set hard against the paler horizon. "Is this the place, Buck?" he called softly. "I think I can smell cattle."

Buck didn't reply. He halted, sat a moment looking southward, then swung out and down, drew forth his booted carbine, and turned to watch Milt do the same. He afterward frowned at their prisoner, his thought obvious. Milt read the look right and shrugged. "We should've cracked his skull back where we found him," he said dispassionately, meaning every word of it. In a land where nature was never mild and her cruel environment formed and sustained the people, to dispatch a rattlesnake of a man like Brownell's wispy killer provoked no regrets, no second thoughts.

Buck leaned his carbine into some brush, went over

to the gunman's saddle, took down the lariat there, and growled for the outlaw to turn his back. He tied the killer's hands behind him, lashed his legs tightly, pushed him face down upon the ground, and rolled him over with his toe. "You let out a bellow," he warned. "Or make any sound at all . . . and I'll kill you, mister. You have my word for it."

Milt, watching all this, stepped up and said to Buck: "I don't like leavin' him behind us like this."

"He can't get loose."

"Well, hell . . . at least gag him."

Buck knelt, yanked off the gunman's neckerchief, stuffed it into the man's mouth, and yanked it tightly with a square knot. As he got up and started back for his carbine, he growled: "Let's go."

Milt stood there, strongly frowning. When Buck was ready to advance, Milt turned protestingly: "I still don't like it. The odds are big enough without leavin' this whelp back here."

Buck looked annoyed. "We need him alive, Milt. I'd kill him in a minute if we didn't need him alive."

"For what, I'd like to know?"

"He talks, Milt. When this one is scairt, he talks. When this is over, we're goin' to need at least one of Brownell's outlaws to testify in court against the others. Now quit squawkin' and come on."

Milt went, but he didn't look mollified. He knew nothing of courts of law. All he was certain of was that Judge Colt and his six lead jurymen were swift and fair and utterly final. In Milt Bond's unwritten book of rules, only fools—and usually dead ones at that—took unnecessary chances. He went along behind Buck, leading his horse, his Winchester in hand, thinking his private thoughts.

They came after a little while to a granite bulwark of jumbled spires and pale bulkheads of solid rock. Here, they caught the first sound of lowing cattle somewhere beyond this mighty rock wall. Here, too, they hid their horses and went on again. Buck, who knew this forlorn place, led out, keeping always to shadows, to sooty little tortured passageways through the rock walls where neither of them could be seen unless a watcher stepped out directly ahead of them.

The sound and scent of cattle became much stronger. Also, there came eventually the aroma of a greasewood fire and cookery. Milt sniffed at this. It had been hours since either of them had eaten. The bouquet of coffee was particularly tantalizing.

The land tilted underfoot. It buckled and broke and lifted again. They went along noiselessly over centuries of gritty dust and ultimately topped out along a series of sharp, small granite parapets. Here, Buck went down to melt into the ghostly shadows and pointed east to where a man sitting cross-legged with his back to them was cradling a carbine in his arms, looking east. Milt shoved up onto all fours preparatory to gliding up behind this renegade, but Buck stopped him, gestured for absolute silence, began edging back down the way they had come, and never once looked back until they'd gotten down into a crevasse a quarter mile away.

As Milt slid down beside him, Buck said: "No, we can't do anything until we get a good look at the main camp. They'd miss that sentry, Milt. It'd be like kicking an ant nest."

They probed for a better passage, found one eventually, and got completely clear of the surrounding rock walls that hemmed in a secret meadow with a good sweet-water spring almost in the exact center of it. Here, with the overhead moon gliding past, they had a good view of what they'd come this far to see—the outlaw camp and the rustled herd of Mexican beef.

Milt, squinting across the grassy place where a cooking fire burnt low and men sat or sprawled or walked aimlessly about, puckered his lips in a silent whistle.

"Must be thirty of 'em," he whispered. "I had no idea there'd be that many." He began wagging his head. "See what you mean," he muttered. "Good thing we didn't knife their sentry."

Buck, studying those shadowy men across the little grassy meadow, said nothing for a long while. He hunkered there with his back to smooth granite, considering this midnight spectacle of wicked-horned Mexican cattle and the half-wild, completely merciless men who had brought them over the line. Eventually he said: "Comancheros, Milt. They're a special breed of men. You never ran across 'em on the north plains. They're the deadliest renegades on earth. They used to trade with the Comanche Indians, but since the Comanches have been reservationed, they've turned to rustling, murdering, robbing . . . anything lawless and profitable. They never go anywhere except in large gangs. They've actually attacked Mexican towns. Texas knows them, too."

Milt eased down beside Buckley. "I've heard tales of Comancheros," he said, staring across the meadow.

"They're whites and Mexicans and Injuns . . . every shade of scum."

Buck said no more about the men. He studied the cattle, estimated their numbers, then glided back into the narrow passageway that they'd used to get this close. Milt followed him, but reluctantly. He was fascinated by that crowd of human vultures over by the campfire.

Buck retraced their way back out of the rocks, made a very careful, wide circle so as not to be detected by that cross-legged sentry, and an hour later got back where their horses were. Here, he turned to explain what course he'd decided upon.

"The Comancheros will go back into Mexico. Brownell's four riders will head the cattle for Tenawa. We can't do anything by ourselves until those two outfits split up."

"You sure some of the Comancheros won't ride along with Brownell's men?"

"No," replied Buck, swinging up over leather, "I'm not sure, but ordinarily, unless the whole band goes somewhere, none of them goes."

Milt also mounted. He said: "Now, I know what was meant when it was said Brownell could bring more men to Tenawa if he needed them. Those Comancheros."

Buck reined around, walked his horse a hundred yards, drew closer to Milt, and shook his head. "I understand things better, too," he explained. "Brownell's cold-bloodedness for one thing. His brazenness for another."

"We got to be damned careful," muttered Milt. "If Brownell gets on to what we're tryin' to do an' brings

127

that murderin' army up to Tenawa. . ." Milt ran the edge of his forefinger across his throat.

They got back to where they'd left their prisoner. Without saying a word they released the outlaw, put him on his horse, and, still wordlessly, started north-ward up the trail again.

For an hour the gunman rode along between Buck and Milt, looking frequently from one to the other. Finally he said: "You saw, didn't you?"

Milt looked around, solemnly nodded, and looked away again.

It was Buck who said, coldly considering the outlaw: "We saw Comancheros."

That was all he said, but anywhere in west Texas it was enough. Comancheros were killed on sight; those who associated with Comancheros, who even knew them, got no mercy.

The gunman's face sweated in the moonlight. He licked his lips and fumbled for words. He had been afraid many times this night but always before there had been at least a glimmer of hope. Now there was none, for even if he cooperated to the extent of inform-ing against Cleve Brownell and Brownell's outlaw crew, because he was a known associate of Co-mancheros he would be hanged or shot. He had only to look on the left of him, on the right of him, to see that this was immutably so.

Buck ordered a stop halfway back. They rested and smoked and said nothing for half an hour, then they went on again. The moon was nearly down by this time. Off in the dingy east the palest kind of watery purple was beginning in an otherwise Stygian sky.

TEN

Buck knew this land. As a lad he'd ridden after cattle with his father and other cowmen the width and breadth of the southward desert. He'd heard most of the grisly tales, had seen many of the unmarked graves, and had met many of the tough Texans who had, over the years, retained their straight-shooting sovereignty here.

Riding now with the tag end of a long night around him and his two dour companions, he traced out in his mind the logical route drovers would use in bringing rustled cattle northward to the plains around Tenawa. He had it in mind to whittle down Brownell's odds a little more. One of Brownell's renegades was already dead. Another was a prisoner, and in view of what had come to light, this one was as good as dead. But there were four more between the Mexican border and Tenawa.

Without prefacing his words with the way his mind was running, Buck said to Milt: "The odds aren't so big. Two to four, Milt, and the four will be pretty occupied keeping those stolen cattle bunched up."

Milt understood. He'd been thinking parallel thoughts. "But we dasn't waste much time. It'll be daylight directly, then it won't be easy at all, cattle or no cattle."

Buck reined west without any explanation. Milt followed along and so did their nameless captive, but he seemed very agitated at what Buck had proposed. "You'll never bring it off," he protested. "You don't know them four fellers. They're old hands on the desert. After sunup they'll spot your trail, sure as hell."

"That," agreed Buck, "is a good point. But on the other hand I'd rather be close to Tenawa in case they've got the Comancheros with 'em."

"They won't have," said the outlaw. "Those fellers don't like coming up here any more. Too many Rangers lookin' for 'em nowadays."

"There'll be only the original four?" queried Milt.

Their prisoner nodded, looking apprehensive. "Listen," he exclaimed strongly, "I've helped you fellers right from the start! I deserve some consideration for that, don't I?"

"You sure do," agreed Milt. "You deserve to die quick instead of slow. Shut up."

Buck kept riding west until he was satisfied, then he halted, sat for a while listening, looked over at Milt, and raised his eyebrows. "No sign of 'em yet," he said. "Stay here with our little friend while I go back a ways and look around."

Milt nodded, got down, and gestured for their captive to do the same.

Buck rode a long mile before he picked up the

sullen lowing of driven cattle. For a while he sat listening to this, then he turned to study that watery far horizon. Dawn would not, he thought, be more than
perhaps two hours off. Whatever they did would have
to be done before sunup. After daylight they could not
hope to get close to Brownell's experienced renegades
in this flat, comparatively open country. He decided to
try and take Brownell's outlaws one at a time, borrow-
ing this time-consuming but usually successful tactic
from the desert Indians who had once ruled this entire
vast wasteland.

Milt was standing with his head to one side when
Buck came riding up out of the gloomy west. Milt
said: "By golly, I think I can hear 'em."

"You can."

Buck dismounted near their captive. He stood for a
moment in thought, then explained to Milt what he had
in mind. Their captive listened critically as though he
were personally involved. He said dispassionately: "It
might work."

This very dispassionate interest moved Milt to
growl—"Don't you have any loyalties at all?"—and
then to glare. After that the renegade said no more.

By riding west Buck and Milt were a long distance
from the northward trail being used by the rustlers.
They remained quietly beside their horses, letting that
oncoming muted bedlam of many moving cattle approach parallel to them. Their prisoner turned pale in
the ghostly night; he was rigidly fearful.

"One at a time," asked Milt, "or both of us together?"

Buck answered this by handing Milt the reins to his
animal and exchanging a long glance with his pardner.

He left his carbine in its boot, took only his lariat and his hip-holstered six-gun. He even bent down, removed his spurs, and buckled them together in the rear rigging ring of his full double-rigged saddle.

"Don't get lost," admonished Milt, looking uneasy. "This whole lousy country looks very much the same to me."

"I grew up around here," assured Buck. "Don't worry." He jabbed a thumb toward their captive. "Watch him. If he tries to yell a warning. . ."

Buck walked due east. He cut in and out of the brush clumps, side-stepped catclaw thorns, slowed when he could faintly make out moving dark red hides against that paling far horizon, and stepped over into the camouflaging gloom of a sage as those great, curved, faintly glowing wicked horns passed as rustled Mexican beeves went plodding along. Under ordinary circumstances these were the most dangerous cattle on earth for a man to be among while on foot. But these were not ordinary circumstances. Buck could see the tucked flanks of those cattle. They had come a long way. They had rested only briefly at Red Rock, not long enough to get all the wrinkles out of their bellies, and they were, along with being tired, also footsore. These things he counted in his favor. Brownell's men could not push this herd. The cattle were too leg-weary to travel faster than a shambling walk.

He moved closer, where trail dust settled across his shoulders, carefully took down the lariat from its place upon his crooked left arm, built a little bear-cat loop— large enough to drop over a man's broad-brimmed hat—and glided from brush clump to shadow to brush clump, getting always closer. Somewhere, on each side of this herd as well as behind in the drag and up front at the point position, were riders.

Those first few animals were past now. The main mob of animals was going by with their shuffling gait, their hanging heads and their little red-crusted eyes. The only foreign sound was a *jangle* of rein chains. It came and went, as though the rider was cutting in and out to keep the animals bunched and moving. Buck, gauging this outlaw's nearness by that jingling little sound, moved quietly to intercept him. Where several yuccas put forth their sword-like columns, straight-standing and in eerie bloom, he halted, catching sight of a rider whose upper body was above that mass of moving shapes.

The horseman seemed unusually alert for this time of night. He was smoking; the little sullen red glow of his cigarette alternatively brightened and dulled out. It was impossible for Buck to make out this man's features clearly, nor did he particularly try. Instead, he concentrated on getting well within roping distance.

The horseman walked his horse along. He sat up there, looking off toward the east across the herd where another rider was paralleling him. He had no inkling of trouble until, with a rising and falling *hiss,* Buck's rope lifted up, hovered, settled suddenly around his neck, and unseated him with a savagely violent wrench.

The renegade emitted a little squawk one second before his breath was fiercely cut off and he went backward off his horse. The animal gave a shying bound, halted, and uncertainly looked back, reins hanging, stirrups still jiggling.

Buck jumped over and pushed his cocked six-gun into the gasping outlaw's chest. The man, with both hands clawing at the rope around his gullet, froze. He stared and choked, muffled a cough and blinked. Buck disarmed him, jerked him upright, and gave him a rough push.

"Get that horse," he snarled at the completely astonished rustler. "Keep your mouth shut."

He had driven his prisoner a hundred feet back toward Milt before the man collected his wits sufficiently to talk. But when he tried, Buck slammed his gun into the outlaw's back, making him wince and gasp. After that nothing was said until Milt sighted them coming along and made a little triumphant grunt.

The outlaw stopped, still with one hand upon his rope-burned throat, and stared hard at the gunman standing there with Milt. The gunman started to speak, but Milt shut him up with a growl.

Buck holstered his gun, looked closely at their fresh prisoner, and wagged his head. "Don't know him," he said to Milt. He began coiling his lariat. "Keep an eye on the pair of them. I'll go get us another one."

Milt protested: "Hey, it's my turn now. You stay and keep an. . ."

"Milt, I know this country. The next one won't be so easy. The herd's gone on by now. There'll be a lot of leg work to do. You might get lost."

This logic made sense to Milt but he continued to stand there, looking glum. Finally he grumbled assent and turned to making a close inspection of their latest prisoner.

Buck was less careful the second time he went forward. There was much less danger of detection now because, except for the drag rider, the rustlers were all at least a half mile ahead of where he came out on their trail.

The rank scent of cattle was thick enough in the still night air to cut with a knife and dust hung above the ground in a kind of alkali mist. Buck trotted ahead through all this until above the drag end of older and slower animals ahead he could clearly make out a man's hat, his wide shoulders, and his thick chest. There looked to be something familiar about this man, but again Buck ignored this for the time being in his concentrating effort to get within roping distance of the drag rider from behind him.

Brownell's man rode loose and slouched. He was neither alert nor interested. He was clearly doing something with which he was contemptuously familiar and which not only bored him but left him drowsy and relaxed.

Buck got within throwing distance, built another little bear-cat loop, planted his feet down hard, and made his accurate cast. He saw the rope drift down, gave it a fraction of a second to settle, then, before the startled horseman completely understood what had happened, Buck took two quick backward steps and jerked the slack. The rustler's plodding horse did the rest; he walked right out from under his rider.

The thickly made outlaw struck down so hard Buck heard wind burst out of his lungs. But this man's coor-

dination was better than average. As Buck ran up, the
outlaw rolled over, dived for his holstered six-gun, and
had it clear of leather before Buck could prevent it.
The man's hand was whipping forward when Buck
sprang. His booted foot came savagely down upon the
renegade's wrist, grinding into sinew and bone with all
Buck's weight bearing downward. The outlaw cried
out, rolled his eyes, and saw that cocked handgun ten
inches from his face and went limp all over, still with
his lips twisted in agony but without a sound passing
them. Buck stepped clear and gestured for his prisoner
to arise.

He now recognized this man as the one who had
been with the smaller gunman in the Baylor barn. The
man's small, muddy eyes, his massively over-balanced
jaw, and his otherwise coarse features were glaringly
familiar even in the poor light. The captive also recognized Buck, but his reaction was quite different. His
little eyes popped wide, his jaw sagged, and he stood
there, blinking in disbelief.

"Get on your horse," ordered Buck.

He followed the man to the waiting, bewildered animal. Afterward he herded him southwesterly with the
unerring instinct of a born desert-range man, and,
when he came along to where Milt was standing with
their other two captives, Buck said: "Take a good look
at this one, Milt. He's an old acquaintance of ours."

The men exchanged a long, sullen look without
speaking. Milt stepped forth to frisk the latest prisoner,
then he said to Buck while assessing the coarse-
featured man: "I want to try this one out."

Before Buck could reply, the small gunman jumped

up in quick alarm and croaked to their latest captive: "Don't fight him, Phil. He broke Thorne's neck with one punch. Honest to God he did. I was right there an' seen it happen."

The coarse-featured, brutish-looking rustler measured Milt from boots to hat. He looked disbelieving but cautious. He was a phlegmatic, slow-witted man with a cruel streak and a perpetual antagonism, but, stupid as he was, he did not overlook Milt Bond's bigness or his quite obvious brute strength. He looked away from Milt, mumbling that he wouldn't fight anyone. Then he sat down beside his acquaintances, putting his baleful, hating gaze on Milt and Buck.

"Still two more of 'em," stated Buck. "But they're too far ahead to go after 'em afoot." He gestured for the captives to stand up. "Sideline 'em," he said to Milt.

They put a lariat around each prisoner's throat, tied their hands behind them, boosted each man into his saddle, then Buck led out, leading the animals in front while Milt rode along behind and a little to one side, holding each of the three lariats in his hand. If any of those outlaws tried to jump off and run or even kick out his horse, all Buck had to do was halt, and all Milt had to do was take a quick dally, set his horse up, and the renegade, coming violently to the end of the rope around his neck, would either snap his spine or choke to death.

None of the outlaws entertained any such notions, though. They were rough, deadly men, but they were not fools. Each of them understood their predicament and went along without a murmur.

Buck set a fast pace and kept at it until he knew they were well ahead of the shuffling herd, then he halted, left Milt with the bound captives, and once more went ahead on foot with his lariat and his six-gun.

ELEVEN

Dawn was nearing, that paling light off in the east was turning from pale-purple to a kind of bottom-of-the-sea bluish-green. This light spread upward and outward over the sky to bring on a dull, metallic brightness that made shapes and distances difficult to assess.

The rustled Mexican cattle were visibly tiring now. It had not only been a long night for them, but, having been driven fast for several days prior to arriving in Texas, they had used up all their reserves of strength. They did not balk but their steady gait became almost a crawl.

Once, as Buck jogged eastward to get on the herd's offside, he heard a man swear exasperatedly at the beasts. This had no effect whatsoever, except perhaps to make the rustler feel relieved of annoyance. But it aided Buck in locating this man, made it possible for him to sweep up through a thicket of sage, spy the onward rider, build his little loop, and stalk Brownell's outlaw.

But the steely first light interceded on the renegade's behalf, at least partially, for as Buck crossed a clearing, took his stand, and made his cast, several long-faced steers saw him, stopped suddenly, threw up their heads and snorted. This unexpected occurrence instantly caught the rustler's attention. He jerked upright, stared at the steers, then dropped his right hand in a flash and swung his head to follow out the direction of those bovine stares.

Here, though, his luck ran out. The noose settled, the outlaw's horse violently jumped, and the man, with his gun half drawn, sailed high and fell hard. But Buck's luck ran out now, too, for that evidently newly broken horse, instead of halting and looking around as an older, more experienced animal might have done, went plunging ahead along the herd's east side, stirrups flopping and reins jerking.

Buck had no time to waste on the horse. He got to where the outlaw was arching up off the ground, dropped his rope, and in a blur of movement drew and aimed. The outlaw was spitting sand; he had alighted face down. He saw Buck's gun and became completely still.

"Drop the pistol!"

The rustler obeyed, then turned to expectorating again, clearing his mouth and pipes of alkali dust and fine-grained sand. Buck looked after the horse. He was nowhere in sight, which greatly heightened Buck's peril. If that stampeding horse kept running north, he would eventually come abreast of the point rider, the last remaining rustler with Brownell's stolen herd. After that it was anyone's guess what would happen, but obviously the point man would drift back to see whether the animal's rider had accidently fallen. He would then find himself quite alone with the herd.

Buck jutted his chin westward and said one sharp word: "Walk!"

They shuffled along with the sound of protesting cattle around them, with the watery light turning a firmer blue color and with the pleasant smell of desert country at first light overcoming the ranker scent of driven cattle. When they got back to where Milt was waiting with the other captives, Buck wasted no time. In short sentences he explained about the horse, ordered their latest prisoner to get up behind one of the other renegades, and mounted his own animal.

Somewhere far out to the east a man's high and questioning cry to another man rose bell-like in the predawn. Buck and Milt exchanged a look and started forward. They rode still farther into the brightening west, then changed course, headed due north, and a half hour before sunup saw Tenawa on the eastern horizon as they made swiftly for the Baylor Ranch.

It was sunup when they cut into the Baylor barn from the misty west. Buck breathed a big sigh of relief as they dismounted inside, pulled their prisoners down, and lined them up. While Milt off-saddled and stalled the animals, forked them feed, and piled the saddles, Buck watched the captives. Only one of those four men was garrulous; the other three were stony-faced and grimly silent.

The coarse-featured man called Phil said: "Baylor, you'll never bring it off. You think Brownell won't know in another hour something went wrong out on the desert? Hell, he'll have riders scourin' this lousy country with fine-toothed combs. I'll make a deal with you . . . turn us loose an' we'll give you a two-hour start for. . ."

"Shuddup," growled big Milt to this outlaw, as he finished with the horses and walked out into the center of the barn, looking high-headed and willing. "Keep your ugly mouth closed or I'll close it for you permanently." He and the man called Phil exchanged a hard look, then Phil dropped his eyes, closed his mouth, and stood there.

"Where'll we hide 'em?" Milt asked Buck. "I suppose what big mouth over there said is true enough . . . Brownell'll be wondering and maybe searching."

Buck flagged toward the yonder yard with his six-gun. "Up at the house," he replied. When Milt would have spoken again, Buck silenced him with an impatient look, gestured for their prisoners to move out, and fell in behind them.

He and Milt herded the renegades around to the kitchen door. Buck's mother was standing grimly there. She had obviously seen them crossing the yard. Her entire attention was focused on the smaller gunfighter. When they halted, she said thinly: "Buck, that's one of the men that came out here to kill your father."

Buck nodded. "I know," he answered. "The other one . . . the one who did the shooting . . . is dead."

"Buckley, I don't want that sort of man in my house."

Milt twisted a troubled expression toward Buck. They were standing out in morning sunlight completely exposed and Milt didn't like it.

Buck cocked his gun, swung it, and Mahalia gasped. "No, not like that!" she cried, running her words together.

"Ma, we can't stand out here. They've got to be hidden. If you don't want him in the house, then I'll have to bury him."

Mahalia stepped aside, the outlaws filed into the kitchen, Milt followed them, and Buck halted beside his mother to put up his gun, run a grimy hand across his face, and say: "It's been a long night."

"I'll fix some breakfast," Mahalia said, still grim in the face, and went on into the house.

Milt took a kitchen chair back to the wall, tilted it up, eased down, and pushed back his dusty hat. Across from him Brownell's renegades stood awkwardly still and silent, shooting glances here and there, never quite meeting Mahalia Baylor's bitter eyes.

It was an uncomfortable breakfast, and, although the renegades undoubtedly were hungry, they did not eat well. Buck and Milt did, though, particularly big Milt, who had an appetite to match his heft. Afterward, Buck drove the prisoners to the pantry and there knelt to pull at an iron ring set in the puncheon floor. A trap door groaned upward and down below lay the dank black hole of a typical west Texas storm cellar. Here, for generations, Texans of the plains country had sought respite from those infrequent but devastating cyclones that swept their countryside, flattening barns and houses, and sometimes even demolishing whole towns.

Without a murmur the prisoners climbed down a spindly little pole ladder, groping with their hands because it was too dark in the storm cellar to see one's hand held up in front of one's face. When the last man was down, Buck knelt, wrenched at the ladder, brought it up, and kicked the trap door closed. Mahalia held forth a large lock. Buck snapped this closed between the iron ring and its accompanying hasp, straightened up, and looked over at Milt.

"This much is finished," he said. "Now there's the rest."

He and Milt returned to the kitchen, helped themselves to another cup of black coffee, stood a while thoughtfully sipping, then looked around as Mahalia spoke to them from the parlor doorway. Her voice, like her expression, was fatalistically sad and bleak.

"It is too late to run now. Brownell will know. He has men ranging the countryside." She looked from her son to Milt and back to her son again. "Last night after you'd left, I had a premonition it would be like this." She brought a hand from behind her, holding a long-barreled revolver. "Don't waste good time, boys. Do what you have to and don't worry about me, or"— she gestured toward the pantry door—"them."

Milt carefully put down his empty cup, hoisted his shell belt, and drew himself up. "Let's go, Buck," he said.

Buckley nodded. "Yeah," he murmured, but made no move, standing there for a little while, gazing over at his mother.

She said: "Where will you go?"

"To Kilgore's. It's the only place. Wyatt tried to organize the cowmen last night, but Brownell got wind of it."

Mahalia inclined her head. "I'm not surprised," she said in that same flat tone. "Buckley, don't take any chances. Now you'd better go. And remember . . . there are spies everywhere." Something in the way she said those last four words made Buck and Milt look closely at her. She let her hand hang down with that horse pistol in it. "We know now about Justin Frazier. Go on, boys, and God go with you."

Mahalia turned back into the parlor, leaving Milt and Buck to exchange a long look, then troop on out into the dazzling morning brightness. Halfway to the barn Milt, gazing out over the range, said: "There's got to be a way of reaching Kilgore's place without being seen."

Buck swung into the barn, said over his shoulder— "There is"—and stopped in his tracks, gazing at the saddles and horses of their prisoners. "We've got to get rid of the horses," he said, strode over, grabbed up two saddles, headed for a hay pile with them, and covered them completely. He and Milt erased all visible evidence that four of Brownell's men had been here by hiding all their gear. Then they rigged out their own animals, freed the rustler's animals, and broke out of the barn in a long lope, driving those loose horses ahead of them.

For an hour they pushed those loose animals northward. Where they unexpectedly came upon a little band of Frazier's Texas Star saddle stock, they hurrahed their prisoners' animals toward them, swung away, and headed for Wyatt Kilgore's ranch in a miles-long big circle that brought them down and around from the far northward plains to the nearest brush thicket above the Fishhook.

Here they dismounted, left their horses concealed, and went ahead to the edge of their shielding underbrush and squatted for a long time, studying the Kilgore ranch yard. The sun was well along on its rising curve toward the meridian by this time, the glass-clear west Texas air sparkled, and coming toward them on an east-to-west course was a slouching rider with a bedroll behind his cantle and a day's beard stubble on his leathery face.

When this man was close enough, Buck recognized him. "Potter," he grunted to Milt. "Brownell's spy that Kilgore said last night he'd sent out to his line shack."

Milt studied the oncoming man for a while. He got both feet under him as Sam Potter came closer to their hiding place, but he neither spoke nor moved. Potter drifted past within three hundred feet, heading for the Fishhook yard. Milt relaxed.

They watched Brownell's man enter the ranch yard, swing down in front of the bunkhouse, remove his bedroll from behind the cantle, and stamp inside with it. As he was returning to the horse, a man appeared up at the main house and called across, his voice easily carrying to Buck and Milt.

"Find the heifers, Sam?"

"Kilgore," breathed Milt. "We're in luck. I thought he might be out on the range with his riders."

Potter called back: "Yep, they were at the water hole! Few of 'em have already calved out. Didn't seem to have had any trouble." Potter turned with his reins in hand. "Where are the boys?" he asked.

Wyatt Kilgore didn't answer right away. He stepped into the yard, sauntering along through deep dust. Just

before he got over to Potter, he said: "They're out, beginning to gather. We've got about a week's branding
and marking to do. They'll be easterly if you want to
go hunt 'em up."

Potter stood there, considering Kilgore. "Any reason why I shouldn't hunt 'em up?" he asked.

Kilgore shook his head. "No reason. They got the
wagon with 'em. You can get fed when you find 'em."
He stopped to watch Potter step up again, turn his
horse, and go leisurely loping eastward out of the yard.

For as long as Sam Potter was in sight neither Buck
nor Milt moved, but, when it was safe to do so, they
both rose up, kicked clear of the underbrush, and
started walking over the intervening distance toward
Wyatt Kilgore.

Buck knew the exact moment when Wyatt saw them
because he stiffened, grew rigid where he stood, and
fixed his surprised, dark stare upon them. For just a
few seconds he remained like that, then he began
swiftly moving toward the barn, gesturing for them to
follow him and to hurry. Both Buck and Milt broke
into the ungainly trot of lifelong horsemen, trying to
make time on foot, and came down into the yard,
swung wide after Kilgore, and ultimately ran in out of
the sunlight where shadowy gloom lay as thick as evening. There, they halted; there, Kilgore called sharply
to them.

"Where did you fellers go last night, where you
been, an' what the devil are you doin' afoot around
here in broad daylight?"

TWELVE

When Buck finished explaining all that had transpired since he and Milt had left the Fishhook the evening before, Wyatt Kilgore felt behind him for the edge of a manger, sank down there, and stared.

"In your storm cellar?" he said. "You got four of Brownell's killers locked in your ma's storm cellar?"

Buck brushed this incredulity aside. "I wish you hadn't sent your men away," he said, speaking almost as rapidly as he was thinking. "We'll need someone to ride into town and see what Brownell's reaction will be to having his stolen Mex cattle drifting all over the range, and only that one cowboy returning from the border with them."

Kilgore closed his mouth, perked up his shoulders as though digesting all that he'd been told, and said: "Hell, that's no problem. I can tell you what his reaction will be. Like tossing a bomb into a church meetin'. Brownell'll round up all his men. . . ." Wyatt suddenly snapped his mouth closed and sprang up off the manger. "Riders," he breathed, his voice full of alarm. "Riders comin' from the south."

He ran past Milt and Buck, peered out of the doorway, stood motionless for a moment, then whipped around, his face tight and his eyes shades darker than they usually were.

"You're goin' to get your answer, boys. That's Brownell and his crew. They're headin' this way in a run armed to the ears." Kilgore looked around, settled his gaze upon a loft ladder, and made a peremptory gesture. "Climb," he snapped. "Get up there, lie down, and for God's sake don't make a sound."

Buck hesitated. It was in his mind that, if Brownell was racing for the Fishhook, it was because his first suspicion involved Wyatt Kilgore and the men who had been in Kilgore's yard the night before.

Wyatt swore at him. "Get up there, dammit. Move!"

Buck moved. Ahead of him big Milt was taking the ladder steps two at a time. All three of them could now hear the drum-roll thunder of horses passing rapidly over summer-baked ground.

In the loft Buck dropped down beside Milt. Beneath them was a deep foot of loose meadow hay, good to smell, good to lie upon, but right now neither comfortable nor comforting. Milt put his lips to Buck's ear and whispered: "Cut off. No way out of here except the way we came up. We're goners, if Brownell gets to snoopin' around."

Buck nodded, lowered his head, and listened as riders jangled down to a halt outside the barn. He heard Wyatt Kilgore go as far as the doorway and say something indistinguishable. Kilgore got back a quick, hard reply in that same deep, rich voice Buck had heard in almost the same spot the night before.

Brownell called out: "Kilgore! I'll give you ten seconds to tell me what you and all those other men were really talkin' about here in your yard last night. Just ten seconds."

Buck held his breath as Wyatt answered, pushing his voice out at Brownell. "We were talkin' about exactly what I told you, Brownell, a roundup. If you don't believe that, I can't help it, but I sent my riders out this morning to begin gathering Fishhook stock, and any other stray cattle they run onto."

This sounded believable. Even Milt, critically listening, nodded his head.

For a moment Brownell said nothing. Buck held his breath. It was agony being where he could not see the outlaw leader and his men. For all Buck knew they were at that precise moment aiming cocked guns at Wyatt, and neither he nor Milt could help Kilgore.

Then Brownell spoke again, some of the testiness gone out of his voice. "All right, but I want the names of those men just the same, Kilgore." Brownell paused. Buck could visualize him turning toward one of his men. Then he said: "Enos, get down and write those names down as Kilgore gives 'em to you." Another pause, then: "Kilgore, I lost Tom Thorne last night and four others. I want those men back an' you're going to help me get 'em back."

"How?"

"Never mind. Give Enos those names. We'll talk about this later."

For a little time the men lying in Kilgore's hay loft heard nothing but the very faint mumble of voices, then Kilgore, speaking loudly, said: "That's all of them, Brownell, but you're wasting your time if you think those men had anything to do with Thorne and the others disappearing."

"Then maybe it was you," snapped the renegade chieftain. "Where you been all night, Kilgore?"

"Right here. So were my riders until I sent them out to commence the gather at sunup this morning. They're on the east range if you want to go ask 'em."

Again Buck thought Kilgore's voice sounded completely believable. So did Milt, who nodded and solemnly winked. Evidently Cleve Brownell also thought this because he said: "Well, somebody around here is moving against me, Kilgore. If not you, then at least it'll be someone hereabouts you know, so you're goin' with us while we hunt 'em down . . . whoever they are."

"How do you know it's anyone at all?" asked Kilgore, speaking up to Brownell. "How do you know Thorne and the others didn't just up and ride off?"

"Thorne, ride off? Hell, Kilgore, you're talkin' like a little child. Those men are outlaws with prices on their heads. The only way they're safe is by stayin' with me . . . and they know that. No, they didn't ride off. You can bet your bottom dollar on that. Something's happened to them and I aim to find out what it is." Brownell's voice dropped a note, turned smooth and iron-like. "The Lord help you Tenawa folks if they're dead, Kilgore. The Lord help you."

Buck turned to gaze over at Milt. There was no mistaking that quiet threat. To the pair of men in Kilgore's loft came the same vision: a powerful Comanchero brigade, racing out of the southward night with guns and ropes and torches. Murder would be the least heinous thing Brownell's henchmen would unleash on the countryside.

Kilgore spoke again, louder this time. Buck, listening closely, had the feeling Kilgore was speaking now for the exclusive benefit of those two men in his loft.

"Who'd try anything against you, Brownell? Hell, the ones who wanted to oppose you the most are dead. Who's left?"

"That Baylor feller for one, Kilgore. And Frank Hardesty. He's got reason. There'll be others. Enos, fetch a horse for Kilgore out of his barn. Make it snappy. We've wasted enough time here."

Buck heard a man moving around down below, his spurs sounding in the barn's cathedral-like emptiness.

Kilgore spoke once more, as loudly as before. "Hardesty's got reason to hate your guts, Brownell, but you broke his heart, and a broken man's got nothing left in him to fight for."

"Maybe. We'll see. As for breaking his heart . . . I wish I'd never seen that damned girl of his. I've had nothing but trouble since I touched her. Enos, hurry up with that horse!"

"As for young Baylor," said Kilgore. "What can one man do?"

"He's got a pardner with him. My boys saw them both."

"All right, what can two men do against you?"

Enos came out of the barn, leading Kilgore's saddle

animal. As he pushed the reins into Kilgore's hand, Brownell said: "Get mounted. We'll find out what Baylor and his friend can do . . . right after we pay a visit to the Hardesty place. Now, shut up and come along."

Buck heard them whip around, lope out of the Fishhook yard all in a rush, then stood to knock away clinging, cured meadow hay. Milt edged over toward the loft ladder, poked his head down, drew it back, and started down.

"All clear," he said.

When they were down out of Kilgore's loft, Milt started for the door in a trot. Buck halted him with one word: "Wait!"

"Wait for what? You heard 'em. They're headin' for the Hardesty place."

"I know, Milt, but we're not. We're headin' for the Baylor place."

Milt scowled darkly. "What the hell?" he said exasperatedly. "We can drift in behind 'em, set up an ambush, an'. . . ."

"The Baylor place, Milt. We don't have enough time to dry-gulch 'em at Hardesty's. They're ridin' fast. We may not even have time enough to set up for them at my place." Buck went past Milt out into the yard. He looked around, then broke over into a run, heading for that distant spot where they'd left their horses.

Milt went after him, looking disgruntled but docile. When they were astride again and zigzagging clear of thorny undergrowth, Buck concentrated so hard on his route away from the Fishhook that he did not see another rider until Milt ran up beside him, pointing dead ahead off in the sunlighted west.

"Horseman, Buck, and he's seen us. He's stopping."

Buck swung his gaze, probing for that rider. He found him and slowed his mount while he watched and waited. But the distant rider sat there, doing nothing, only considering him and Milt.

For a little this impasse continued, then Milt said: "We dasn't leave someone around here to say he saw us ride away from Kilgore's place. If that word gets back to Brownell, Wyatt Kilgore's as good as dead."

Buck agreed to this. He set his horse toward the watching horseman far out and booted him over into a lope. When they were close enough to make out a scarlet shirt, Milt blew out a big breath.

"It's a girl. Hell's bells, Buck, it's that Frazier girl."

Buck had already surmised this. He slowed again, rolling his brows inward and downward in perplexity. He thought it entirely unlikely Kathleen had any inkling of the trouble scouring the countryside, let alone her father's part in it. But on the other hand, one slip from her to old Justin, or anyone else for that matter, and Wyatt Kilgore would die.

"We'll take her along," he said aside to Milt as they came closer and Kathleen, recognizing Buck, raised her arm in a warm gesture. "I'd give a section of good land to have avoided this meeting, but it's too late now, so we'll have to take her along."

They came up and drew rein. Kathleen's smile faded a little at the sight of those two. They were dirty and whiskery and grim-faced. She shot big Milt a bewildered glance, then put her liquid large eyes fully upon Buck.

"What is it?" she asked. "Buck, what's the matter? You look . . . fierce."

Buck swung his head, nodded, and Milt eased forward, caught Kathleen's reins, straightened back, and turned his mount, leading off. Kathleen's face underwent a sudden change. It showed alarm and something else, something Buck could not exactly define, but which made him inwardly wince.

"Buck . . . what are you doing?"

He nodded again at Milt. The three of them broke over into a swift lope, bearing far out around the Texas Star range. Hot afternoon sunlight burnt down upon them. A kind of smoke-like heat haze softened the far-out distances, and mica dust in the air reflected into their eyes. Buck pushed up beside Kathleen to speak. She stared at him out of a stunned and completely bewildered face.

"There's been trouble," he said crisply. "Brownell is looking for me and for my pardner here. Kathleen, I'm sorry, but this is the only way. You'll have to stay with us for a while."

"Trouble?" she asked, looking confused, looking anxious. "Buck, I wouldn't tell Cleve Brownell I saw you. . . ."

"I know you wouldn't. That is, I think you wouldn't. But Kathy, we just can't take the chance, an' we don't have a lot of time to explain."

"Buckley, if you'd just asked me . . . I'd have come along with you."

He flinched from that reproach and looked away, then back again. "All right, Kathy . . . then I'm asking you."

She scowled over at him, some of the bewilderment fading. "Tell *him*," she said heatedly, motioning toward Milt, "to give me back my reins."

Milt looked over. Buck made a little wry face and bobbed his head. Milt slowed, drew in, swung Kathleen's reins over the head of her moving horse, and held them out. She took them, adjusted them, and, when Milt set the running pace again, she kept even with Buck, saying nothing more, her full-lipped mouth a little flat, her large, grave eyes kindling with indignation, and her expression granite-like.

They went far out around Texas Star, then dropped due southward again, making the run to the Baylor place without difficulties. As they neared the barn, Kathleen turned her warm glance upon Buck and said in a quite practical way: "If you're in trouble, Bucky, you shouldn't come here."

Buck made no reply to this. They rocketed right up to the barn's rear doorway before slowing, then Buck hit the ground one jump ahead of Milt, swung to offer Kathleen a hand—which she ignored to alight unassisted—and the trio of them passed on out of sunlight into cool and fragrant barn gloom.

Kathleen was a little breathless. Her radiant hair was no longer perfectly in place and her flushed cheeks, aroused eyes, and strong breathing showed a kind of excitement Buckley had never before seen in her. She was, suddenly and stunningly, beautiful in his sight.

THIRTEEN

They went to the house, passed into the kitchen from the rear, and met Mahalia. She said: "I saw you coming." She let her gaze linger upon Kathleen only a moment. Her real interest and attention were for her son. "What's happened?"

Buck explained about Brownell and Kilgore, but he was reluctant to talk, crossed to the stove, poured himself a cup of coffee, and motioned for Milt to do likewise. For this moment he forgot about Kathleen Frazier.

Milt asked Mahalia how their prisoners were. Mahalia said she'd fed them, that they'd offered her five thousand dollars to release them, and throughout this exchange Kathleen stood there, looking and listening and faintly frowning.

Buck finished the coffee. He stood a moment, looking over at Justin Frazier's daughter. "Stay in here with Ma," he told her. "Brownell's coming with his crew. They'll have Wyatt Kilgore with them as a prisoner. You stay out of sight." He swung half around. "Ma, if there's shooting, stay away from the windows, keep out of sight."

"Son, what can you two do against Cleve Brownell and his killers?"

Buck jerked his head at Milt. The pair of them went as far as the back door. There, Buck said: "You'd be surprised at what we can do together. Up in Dodge City we surprised a whole town. Remember what I told you." Milt passed on outside, but Buck, considering Kathleen again, was struck with a notion. He seemed about to say something about this, but in the end he only looked over at his mother, nodded, and silently left the house.

They walked back to the barn, got into shade there, and Milt, thinking unique thoughts, muttered: "That girl doesn't know anything, Buck. I'd stake my saddle on it."

A horse blew its nose out a little distance from the barn's rear opening, and, if Buck had intended to take up the discussion of Kathleen Frazier, he instantly forgot it at this sound. He and Milt snatched up carbines, padded swiftly to vantage points along the rear wall, and peered out.

A solitary horseman was approaching out there. If he'd been riding along in the same direction he was now facing, he'd have come straight across the Texas Star.

"Who is he?" asked Milt, squinting out where that steadily approaching rider was approaching.

"Justin Frazier," replied Buck. "The last person we need around here right now."

Milt twisted to scowl and say: "Well, he's here. What you figure we ought to do?"

Buck, already considering this, swung away, eased down on a manger, and scratched his head. "Dunno," he growled. "If we talk to him, which we'll have to do now, and let him ride off . . . he'll likely come across Brownell and tell him we're waitin' here in the barn."

"Keep him here," said Milt, taking a last long look at the nearing rider. "Toss him down in that storm cellar with the others."

Buck looked up. "An' how do we explain that to Kathleen?" he demanded.

Milt pursed his lips and furrowed his brow. Then his face suddenly brightened. "Tie him up an' keep him in the barn with us. She'd never know then."

Buck got up, walked over, leaned his carbine out of sight, and stepped across the threshold for Justin Frazier to see. Milt remained where he was in barn gloom, his carbine held across his body with both hands.

Frazier spied Buck at once, altered his course which had been set for the main house, and walked along, reins swinging, shoulders slumped under the afternoon heat, his craggy old face shadowed by his hat brim and unreadable. When he was close, Frazier halted, crossed both hands upon the saddle horn, and sat a moment, just looking. Finally he spoke.

"Why are you staying, Buckley. It will only get you killed."

"I'd like to ask *you* a question, Mister Frazier. Why do you let Kathy ride out alone, with things the way they are?"

"Why not?" countered Frazier. "She's a heap sight safer than you are."

Buck interpreted this to mean that Frazier had some

kind of an agreement with Cleve Brownell. He stood there blank-faced, studying this old cowman of wealth and power, still having difficulty accepting what he knew of Frazier to be fact.

"Come in out of the sun," he said, making his tone casual and keeping that impassive look on his face. "Maybe you heard . . . there was trouble last night."

Frazier didn't move at once. "Trouble? What kind of trouble?"

"Brownell lost five men."

Frazier was startled. "What? Lost five men how?"

Instead of replying, Buck stepped back into the barn and beckoned. Frazier brushed his mount's ribs with spurs. The beast walked ahead, stepped inside the barn, and halted from slight rein pressure. Frazier got stiffly down.

"What kind of trouble, Buckley. I hadn't heard anything."

Buck faced around with his six-gun, held low and steady. He said nothing at all. Frazier's eyes popped wide. Milt glided forth from shadows, disarmed the old cowman, and stepped away. Buck put up his gun.

"Tom Thorne is dead," he told Frazier. "Four of Brownell's men are prisoners . . . and within the next half hour or so Brownell will come ridin' into this yard with his remaining killers."

Justin Frazier seemed more demoralized by this grim announcement than he was to find himself obviously a captive of Buck Baylor and some big, darkly dressed man, standing back there with a carbine, who he had never seen before. He dropped the reins of his horse, looked right, looked left, and licked his lips.

"Then it *was* you!" he exclaimed. "I rode over to ask your ma if she knew anything about some loose saddle critters I found with my remuda a couple of hours ago. I thought it might have been you put them horses with mine." Frazier peered around at Milt, took the big man's careful measure, looked back at Buck, and went on speaking. "Those horses got Mex brands on 'em. I thought they had to belong to some of Brownell's men. No one else around here rides Mex horses. They got saddle stains of sweat on 'em, too, and they been rid a long ways."

"You're pretty observant," drawled Milt.

Buck said sardonically to his pardner: "More observant than you think, Milt. The reason he rode over here was because he didn't want Brownell to find those horses with his animals. Otherwise Brownell, who trusts no one, might think Frazier was double-crossing him."

Milt's even white teeth shone in a tough smile. "I wonder what Brownell will think now . . . the missing men's critters in with old Frazier's remuda?"

Justin peered around at Milt again. "Is that where those blamed horses came from? You fellers turned 'em loose with my stock." The craggy old face swung back frontward. "Buckley, you did that on purpose. You're trying to get me killed."

"At the time all we wanted to do was get rid of those animals," retorted Buck, "but now it's beginning to look like we've got a guardian angel, after all, Justin. The best way to beat a combine like you and Brownell is to divide you. I think we've done that, even though it was an accident."

Frazier's face hardened against Buck. His faded, pale eyes became wintry. "Even if that's what you've done, it's not going to save your hide, Buckley. Nor your pardner's hide, either, if the brace of you've crossed Brownell. Whatever he does to me . . . he'll do twice as bad to you."

Buck drew in a big breath. He let it out. "I think the hardest thing for me to get used to, Justin, is what you've turned out to be. I'm glad, in a way, my pa isn't around to see that."

Frazier puckered his eyes. He looked over Buck's head and he said with the testiness suddenly gone out of his voice: "I'm an old man. I've fought all my life. Something goes out of a man when he gets old, Buckley. I'm not excusing myself. I'm only trying to hang on so there'll be something for Kathleen when I go."

Buck turned away. With his back to Frazier he said: "My pa wasn't a young man, either. He'd fought all his life, too. But he knew I wouldn't want anything from him better than his honor. Milt, tie him up, dump him out of my sight somewhere."

Buck walked away from Frazier, went as far as the barn's front door, looked out, saw nothing but the dazzling brilliance of early afternoon without dust or movement anywhere, and turned back when Frazier called out to him.

"Buckley, don't do this! Listen to me. Brownell will find those horses."

"Of course, he will."

"You don't understand. Kathy is out riding somewhere. If Brownell doesn't find me to take his wrath out on, he'll find her." Frazier writhed until Milt swore at him, ordered him to stand still until he was tied. Frazier cried out again, not heeding Milt at all.

"Buckley, you know what Brownell does to girls. Think of Frank Hardesty's daughter . . . think of my Kathy. Don't let it happen again. Listen to me. I'll give you money."

Buck said: "And if we turned you loose, what could you do against Brownell? You're an old man, Justin. Brownell would eat you in one mouthful."

"No. I could find Kathy and flee with her. We could. . ."

"You couldn't get a mile away before Brownell's hawks would swoop down on you. You're like the rest of us, Justin . . . you ran out of time about sunup this morning."

Milt finished tying the old cowman. He stood back, critically examining his handiwork, then he stepped in, bent, encircled Frazier with his mighty arms, lifted and walked across the barn to a corner where harness hung. There he bent Frazier in the middle, sat him with his bound hands and his back against a solid, thick wall, and turned his back to stroll up to where Buck was leaning.

"Tell him," he said in a low voice. "It's all right to despise a man of his stripe, but not to torture 'em. Tell him we got his doggoned daughter an' she's over yonder in the house with your ma."

Buck looked sardonic. "You think that'd ease his worries, Milt? Hell, it'd make 'em worse. He knows Brownell's coming here. He knows there's only you and me to oppose Brownell. And his girl is over in the house with no one to protect her but my ma." Buck wagged his head back and forth. "Tell him, if you want, I won't. The least torture for Frazier now is believing his daughter's ridin' out somewhere where she at least has a chance to run."

Milt screwed up his face, wrinkled his brow, and dolefully wagged his head. He peered out and around and drew in his head to concentrate on making a smoke. They stood like that for a long time with the moments crawling by. When Milt had his cigarette going, he deeply inhaled, exhaled, went back after his carbine, returned to the front barn entrance, and hunkered there, his eyes drawn out speculatively, shrewdly narrow and thoughtful.

Buck, heeding nothing but that still, empty and sunlighted, flowing land, spoke aloud a thought he had. "I wish we'd heard Kilgore name the others to Brownell when we were over at his place in the loft."

"Didn't you recognize 'em last night in Fishhook's yard?" asked Milt, from his squatting position.

"No . . . only a couple of the cowboys. It was too dark and things happened too fast."

"It wouldn't help us now, anyway," said Milt, stubbing out his smoke and standing up to flex his legs and make a big sweep of the empty land. "What we need right now is a company of Texas Rangers . . . or a Gatling gun."

Time ran on, the sun dipped off toward a distant merging with the earth's rind, turning faintly red, and a little vagrant breeze ran into the barn from the west, carrying with it the familiar tar-weed, sage, and buckbrush scent of the range.

Over at the main house there was no visible movement, no audible sound. Buck thought of his mother over there, and of Justin Frazier's long-legged, lovely daughter. He thought of another girl, too, and wrenched his mind away from the agony this recollection brought.

Milt came unexpectedly to break in upon his somber thoughts with a statement: "We'd better concentrate on the men closest to Kilgore," he mused aloud. "Even Brownell isn't as important to us as Kilgore."

Buck nodded.

Milt saw the lack of enthusiasm of this nod and said softly: "I know. I know how you feel about Brownell. He hasn't done anything personal to me . . . but just on general principles I'd like to spread-eagle him over an ant hill. Still, we'll settle his hash in due time. Right now it's Kilgore's hide we've got to drag out of this mess in one piece. We don't need any more enemies right now. What we need is a few good allies."

"Well," murmured Buck, standing like stone with his carbine in hand, staring far out through narrowed eyes, "we're going to get our chance to fish or cut bait pretty quick now, Milt. Look there, off to the west an' a little southward."

Milt looked, turned still all over, and watched a faint dust banner beat up into sizable proportions as a body of hard-riding horsemen swung onward toward the Baylor place from the direction of Tenawa. "Won't be long now," he muttered, turned, and threw a quick look over where their bound and gagged prisoner was staring from frantic eyes at the pair of them. "But if you think we're in trouble, think of Frazier. Whether we win or lose, he loses."

FOURTEEN

They counted the oncoming horsemen. Including the leader, who rode on ahead a few feet, there were six riders. Softening sun glow sparkled off belt buckles, bits, spurs, rifle plates, and holstered handguns. A seventh man, sandwiched between two others, was farther back. This one rode with an awkward ungainliness.

"Kilgore," breathed Buck. "They've tied his arms behind him."

Milt squatted across the barn doorway from Buck. He hefted his Winchester once, then grew still, just watching.

Brownell came close enough to be recognized. He was within easy carbine range before he slowed, raised an arm to slow the others, and racked down into a steady walk as he came closer to the Baylor Ranch yard.

Milt spoke briefly, without taking his eyes off those renegades and their chieftain. "The two on either side of Kilgore. You take the left one. I'll take the right one."

"All right," retorted Buck, fading back from sight of

166

the approaching riders. "But wait . . . be damned sure before you open up."

"The odds aren't so bad, after all," said Milt, then said no more.

Cleve Brownell's thin-featured, hard, and shrewd face came over the distance to Buck, striking a deadly chord somewhere deeply within him. This was the man who had taken Carol, used her, and turned his back on her. This was also the man who had ordered his father's execution.

Sweat ran under Buck's shirt; it trickled across his forehead and stung his eyes. He had to force his eyes off Brownell long enough to study the men with him. Those six were a ruthless-looking lot, unclean in their personal appearance, dissipated, tough, and unrelenting. Each one of them was a killer. Even from a distance of a thousand yards this was glaringly apparent. Buck knew the type. He'd encountered many of them on the trail and in the trail towns—vicious, deadly human wolves, men who killed for money or for fun. He lifted his carbine, snugged it gently back, rested one elbow on one knee, and let the party of outlaws get well within range.

"Like shootin' fish in a rain barrel," said Milt, and cocked his carbine.

From back in his dark place Justin Frazier, forgotten for these last few minutes, had worked loose his gag by chewing. He was straining mightily at the rope binding his arms behind him, but this had not been carelessly tied. He could make no headway at freeing his arms at all.

Ahead, every word that passed between Buck and

Milt carried easily back to old Justin. He knew how close Brownell was, knew how many men were out there riding into the yard with him, knew without hearing a thing when Buck and his pardner had the outlaws down their carbine barrels. And old Justin threw back his head and let off a resounding scream of warning. The words of this roar were unintelligible but the alarm in Frazier's voice was vivid enough.

Buck, concentrating ahead where Brownell was riding into the yard, jumped at Frazier's yell. So did Milt. Out in the yard Brownell's head flung toward the barn and his rein hand automatically yanked back. He was a man who had survived this long only because of instantaneous reflexes. Now, without a word to his men, Cleve Brownell dropped far over the side of his animal, spun the beast, and sank in the hooks. Milt fired at that second. A breath later Buck also fired. The man on Wyatt Kilgore's right side flung up his arms, grew rigid, then, as his frightened mount sprang ahead, the stricken rider fell heavily. A second later the man on Kilgore's left, who had been instinctively ducking, caught Buck's slug through the top of his head. He kept right on bending over, all the way, struck the rump of a horse ahead of him, which scooted ahead in a duck-tailed jump, letting the man go head down into the rising dust.

The gunfire blew up in a twinkling as Brownell's remaining renegades fought their horses around in a wild effort to break clear of this obvious ambush, turning the yard gray-blue with gunsmoke and a deafening kind of handgun thunder.

Buck swung to seek Brownell. Two slugs cut wood a foot from him, making him flinch and suck back deeper into the barn. Across from him Milt was firing, levering, and firing. He was cool and deliberate and unhurried at his work.

A horse, spinning clear, shuddered in mid-jump, dropped its head, and hit the ground, cartwheeling its rider head over heels. The horse was dead before it fully struck the ground, a bullet through its brain. The man rolled frantically to get clear. Two outlaws raced past him; neither bent to offer an arm up. They left the unhorsed renegade standing there, looking confused. He got control of himself, though, in a flash, dived down behind the dead horse, pushed up his pistol, and snapped off two shots into the barn.

Another outlaw, calmer than his companions, had sufficient sense not to do as Brownell had done—not try to out-distance bullets by fleeing eastward. This man whipped around westerly, cutting himself off from Buck's sight in two big jumps, and angled so as to come upon his enemies from the rear.

Cleve Brownell, who had moved first and fastest, got miraculously out of Winchester range. Two of his men spurred frantically out toward him. Buck and Milt were concentrating on those two, unconscious of the peril stalking them from behind, until a gun exploded at the barn's rear, making a crashing echo inside. Both men dropped flat and rolled. Over where the harness lay, Justin Frazier, also alarmed by this flanking fire, tipped himself over. His feet struck a length of chain tug, setting it to rattling. The renegade in the rear doorway was diverted by this sound. He swung out of his gunfighting crouch, faced off to his left a little, and got off two shots.

Buck, belly down in the dust, fired at the exposed man in back. He'd abandoned his carbine the minute it was evident one of Brownell's killers had flanked them, was in the barn, and his six-gun made its shattering roar, sounding altogether different from the second shot to come from up front. He heard Milt's carbine but did not look around. He was intently watching the crouching man.

Milt fired again. The gunfighter seemed grabbed from behind and jerked backward. He dropped his gun, beat air with two flailing arms, then turned and drew himself fully upright and started quite steadily out of the barn. Buck was thumbing back the dog of his six-gun, steadying it upon the man, when, without an outcry or an uneven step, Brownell's renegade suddenly bent over and slid face down into the churned earth, red now from the dying daylight.

It was all over except for the hidden gunman potting into the barn from behind the dead horse. Buck, with his handgun, turned, saw Milt taking careful aim, and held his fire. Milt squeezed off his shot. The unseen man's hat violently jumped up from behind that dead horse, then sank down. Milt lowered his weapon, peered cautiously out, found nothing perilous, and started to stand up. Abruptly that unseen outlaw threw up his arm, raised his head, and swung his pistol to bear. Milt, off balance and for the space of a breath unable to do anything, hung there.

Buck fired, thumbed back, and fired again. The outlaw's head went violently backward. His gun exploded, plowing up dust for twenty feet ahead of him where the bullet dug in. The man rolled and flopped

170

and tumbled out into plain sight, lying upon his back with both arms outflung.

Milt gingerly finished straightening up. He looked far out where Brownell and his two surviving riders sat a long way off. Buck, across from him, was also coming upright. He leaned aside his Winchester, removed his hat, and beat dust from his clothing, then he ignored Milt to look northward where a man was writhing in clouds of dust, kicking and tossing and cursing. The unmistakable wispiness of Wyatt Kilgore, as well as the identifiable vinegariness of his profanity, said emphatically that Kilgore had survived injury and was violently opposed to lying out there any longer, trussed like a turkey.

"Cover me," said Buck, starting out into the yard.

"Yeah," called Milt. "And Buck . . . thanks!"

Buck twisted, made a little crooked smile, and kept on walking. Far out, Cleve Brownell and his surviving outlaws, seeing it was all over back down there in the Baylor yard and no others would be coming out to join them where they were, whipped around and went loping off toward Tenawa.

Buck knelt, brought forth his knife, and sawed away at the hard-twist lariat rope holding Wyatt Kilgore. He stoically ignored the cowman's writhings and rantings until he'd freed Kilgore, then he got up, helped Kilgore up, and said: "Shut up!"

Kilgore's jaw snapped closed. He looked fiercely at Buck, looked out where Brownell had gone, ran his gaze over two dead men and one dead horse in his sight, and let out a big breath.

"They had no idea you'd be here. They were comin' to take your ma hostage." Kilgore saw Milt step out.

He ran an unsteady hand through his hair. "Close," he muttered as Milt went over, toed the dead renegade gently, then started over. "Damned close, Buckley."

"They'd have killed you anyway, Wyatt."

"Sure they would've, but I could've gotten killed by accident by one of you fellers, too, you know, an' a dead man is just as dead, whether by accident or on purpose."

"Wyatt, what did they do over at Hardesty's place?"

"Nothing. Frank was down on his hands and knees cleanin' a hen house. Brownell just looked at him, made a distasteful face, and left. I guess he couldn't stand the sight o' Frank Hardesty any more than Frank can stand the sight of him."

Milt went back into the barn without coming over to them at all. Kilgore looked after him. He shook his head and rubbed his jaw and said: "We got to move, Buck. We got to get ridin'."

"What are you talkin' about? Ride where?"

Kilgore's dark eyes flashed with irritability and swift impatience. "Ride where? You idiot, where do you think? One of us has to go round up my riders and the men who were at my place last night. We've got to move fast. Brownell's bad hurt after what happened here. He's only got two, maybe three or four men left. The countryside's never had such a chance like this to break him. We got to all rise up, band together, and grind him into the dust before he can get help."

Buck suddenly started. The Comancheros! Brownell would send for those Comancheros, and they wouldn't be but one night's ride south into Mexico, if they'd be that far. It was entirely possible they'd remained at the Red Rock camp overnight. If that were so, then one of Brownell's remaining men could kill a horse getting down there, kill another one coming back—with something like thirty-five of the worst, bloodiest killers known in the West behind him.

He took hold of Kilgore's arm to prevent the cattleman from going toward the barn for a saddle animal. He told him of his fears that the Comancheros might be only a three- or four-hour ride southward, that Brownell would surely send for them, then he released the darker, smaller man, letting Kilgore absorb this.

For a moment Kilgore said nothing, but obviously his mind was moving now at top speed. "All right," he snapped. "All right, I'll tell you how I think we ought to work this. I'll hightail it for my crew. I'll split the boys up, send 'em to every ranch around here to fetch the cowmen together in town. You and your pardner go after Brownell's messenger. Try to get him before he gets to the Comancheros. If you can't do that, Buck, come back to Tenawa as fast as you can. We'll need every man and every gun."

"Your men are out on the east range, Wyatt."

"I know that, dammit. It'll be almighty close . . . whether we can spread the word and get organized in time, or not. That's why you and Milt had better head out right now."

Buck nodded, turned, and started for the barn. Kilgore, with equal determination but shorter legs, had almost to trot to keep up.

They stepped through pre-dusk, past the sprawling renegade beside the dead horse. The first man to fall, and the second one, were also being blessedly dimmed out by the settling gloom. But as they entered the barn,

Milt raised up from where he was straightening out two more bodies. Buck stopped dead, still looking at the heavier, older of those two.

Milt looked up. He motioned toward the renegade he'd killed with his Winchester. "When he was standing in the doorway," he murmured, "I saw him twist and throw a couple over where some chain harness was jingling. That's when he must've gotten old Justin."

Wyatt Kilgore was just as stunned as Buck. He bent over to stare intently into the gloom. He straightened back and said: "Dead as a post, Buck. Old Justin Frazier's dead."

Buck had nothing to say. He knelt, cut loose the bonds securing Frazier's ankles and arms, put the corpse in an upright position, and placed his own fired-out Winchester in Justin's stiffening fingers. "Milt," he said to his pardner, "drag that renegade out of here so it'll look like all Brownell's men died out in the yard . . . and so it'll look like Justin died in here fightin' 'em with you and me."

Milt's troubled expression faded. He bent, and Kilgore helped him. They got rid of the dead outlaw, went back, and stood there with Buck, surveying Justin Frazier, who looked for all the world as though he'd died, gun in hand, defending the Baylor barn.

"Kathleen must never know how it really was, you two," said Buck. "Agreed?" Both Kilgore and Milt solemnly nodded.

FIFTEEN

Buck and Milt left the Baylor place on fresh mounts without taking even the few minutes it would have required to go first to the house. They rode southeast so as to cut in behind any rider Brownell might have sent from Tenawa after the Comancheros.

It was too dark to pick up tracks, which annoyed Milt, so they rode steadily for an hour, then halted to listen, to dismount, press their ears to the ground, and strain to pick up reverberations. Neither of them heard a thing.

"Maybe," suggested Milt as they were scudding southward again, "Brownell didn't send for those Comancheros."

Buck was more than skeptical of this. "He's fighting for his life, Milt. He'll do everything he can, including bringing in outside help if he can get it."

They covered a number of miles before halting again, getting down to plumb the ground for echoes. This time Buck heard the faintly distant cadenced hoof falls he was hoping for.

He drew back. "You hear 'em, Milt?"

"Yeah, but he's a long way ahead of us. Maybe a mile."

Again they hastened onward. The land began to glow with nocturnal iridescence. Darkness fell swiftly as it ordinarily does on the summertime desert, but the occasional yucca blossoms, the other pale and delicate flowers, retained a ghostly paleness long after the sun had set.

Sand gave way to flaky soil with pebbles in it, and this in turn began to strengthen into stony earth with infrequent large stones, lying scattered. They were getting down near the border. Buck rode along comparing distances. He knew this country well, knew its idiosyncrasies and its pitfalls. The one that troubled him most now was its acoustically clear and bell-like air. A gunshot, for instance, would carry miles, the echo easily outdistancing the bullet itself. He looked over at Milt.

"I hate to do this to the horses, but, unless we can overtake him within the next mile, we'll have to give up and head back. There'll probably be shooting. If there is, those Comancheros will hear it if we get much closer to their camp before getting Brownell's messenger."

Instead of speaking to Buck, Milt explained the entire situation to his horse, apologized for the necessity, and hung in his hooks. The beast gave a startled leap and lit out in a hard run.

They covered half a mile in a matter of a very few minutes. It occurred to Buck that they should listen again, but he pushed this notion aside. They did not have the time for more delays. It was a nearly fatal decision, for any renegade worth his salt used the same method for determining whether or not he was being followed, and Brownell's outlaw was no exception. He'd listened, had picked up the oncoming roll of two pursuing riders, and had swiftly faded out westward. Milt was nearest to him when the pair of pursuers swept up on him. The outlaw steadied his gun and fired.

Milt's big-brimmed hat sprang into the air like some enormous, astonished bird and went sailing wildly off into the night, its owner flinching from that near meeting with death, while on his left Buck Baylor hauled back, drew his gun, and swung his horse all in one blur of movement. He fired at the muzzle blast he'd caught from the corner of his eyes, fired twice, then booted his animal straight at that unseen renegade. With a roar of anger Milt fought his frightened mount around, hauled out his handgun, and went charging after Buck.

Brownell's messenger had evidently thought he could down both his pursuers before they could become organized against him. He'd made a bad miscalculation. In fact, he'd made two grave mistakes. The first one was to fire at all. He might have tried to avoid his pursuers. But it was the second error of judgment that put him now in the unenviable position he found himself in. He whipped around to race southward. Behind him was the clear sound of a running horse and the abrasive rub of leather on leather. He twisted, fired, hooked his horse, and ran on a hundred feet. Three unevenly spaced bullets came searchingly in his wake, his horse faltered, stumbled, ran on another fifty feet, then fell heavily and lay still.

"He's down!" called Buck. "He's afoot."

Milt yanked back, hit the ground, ran to a brush clump to secure his horse, and afterward stood a moment reloading. During this interval Buck came along and also swung down.

"Split up," he said. "You take the east and I'll take the west. Nail him any way you can, but nail him. He'll try making it on foot."

Buck reloaded as he trotted southward, dodging in and out of brush patches. For a little while he could hear big Milt hurrying away, off to his left.

The renegade's dead horse lay where faint star shine touched it. The animal was on its side, all four legs extended. It looked as though it were resting. The saddle was askew, but what held Buck's attention longest, as he passed the animal, was the empty saddle boot. Their enemy had yanked out his Winchester, had taken it with him, which gave him superior fire power over Buck and Milt who had only their six-guns.

For a while there was a deep silence. The night ran on and nothing out there seemed changed from the beginning of time. The land, the undergrowth, the overhead pale-lighted ancient sky. Buck passed along slowly, feeling the eeriness of this stalk, feeling the peril and the deadliness.

Off in the east Milt's unmistakable roar sounded a fraction of a second ahead of a gunshot. Buck stopped dead, still trying to figure what those nearly simultaneous sounds meant. Milt could have stumbled upon their enemy, cried out, and fired at the same time, or it could have been the renegade's shot, a second after being sighted by Milt.

The fact that there was no second shot prompted Buck quickly to change course, go hastening eastward toward those sounds. Silence built up around him. It formed an almost physical barrier. As before, this gloomy, ghostly desert world was still and breathless and faintly lighted.

Buck halted when a sixth-sense warning jangled out along his nerve ends. He stood in the ragged shadow of a bushy brush clump, testing the roundabout night. For a long while he stood without moving. There was something wrong here.

A man's rapidly running footfalls suddenly sounded ahead and a little south of Buck. He'd heard Milt Bond's spurs too many times not to recognize that the sounds he now heard were not being made by his pardner. He had a bad moment. Brownell's messenger was fleeing southward. Within a matter of minutes he'd be far enough south so that by firing his gun he could alert the encamped Comancheros to imminent danger. On the other hand, it was possible that Milt had stumbled onto the outlaw, had cried out probably in that very brief second when he saw the renegade's gun bearing down upon him, and was now lying somewhere close by, perhaps badly injured.

The decision actually was already made for him, but it was not an easy one to abide by. One man, no matter how close to Buck, could not stand between his going after the outlaw and thus seeking to protect an entire countryside including many women rather than hunting Milt. He struck out to the south in a quick trot. He was not cautious nor had he time to be. It was bad enough trying to find a forewarned renegade in the darkness, trying to escape, without trying to do this slowly and cautiously.

He did not find the man. He ran south, then swung back and forth, traveling east and west, hoping to cut his trail in this manner. But nearly a half hour later he had to stop, had to admit defeat. While he was standing there, taking one last, long measure of the desert night, two sudden gunshots sounded a goodly distance to the south. There was a pause, then two more quick shots.

Obviously this was a signal. There was no one down where that renegade was firing who might be his enemy. Therefore, he was signaling either his approach to the Comancheros, or was calling for their aid. Either way, Buck thought, the Comancheros would hear those shots, would come to investigate, and the best thing he could now do would be to find Milt and get out of there before he was the pursued instead of the pursuer.

He retraced his steps to the spot he'd stood earlier, near the thriving brush clump, called Milt's name several times, and went carefully, moving back and forth. It was a long search but he found Milt. A moment ahead of this Milt called huskily. When Buck came around a green-barked, stunted paloverde tree, Milt, with his broad back to this spindly support, looked upward. Dull star shine reflected sullenly off a scarlet stain the size of a man's palm upon Milt's upper right leg. Buck knelt.

"You find him?" asked Milt, and called the renegade who had escaped a savage name.

"No. Can you walk?"

"I got to," growled Milt. "It's not a question of whether I can or not. I got to. Here, give me a hand up."

Buck leaned, caught hold, and straightened back. Milt was like lead, but he rose up, balanced upon one leg, and ground his teeth. He tentatively tested his injured leg, swore with feeling, bent over to probe his wound, then looked up, his face clearing, looking greatly relieved, almost joyful.

"Man, I thought the danged thing was busted."

"Isn't it?"

"No," answered Milt, and eased his weight down again. "Lookee there. Punctured a little but not busted."

"We've got to get out of here. Brownell's man fired off a signal."

"Well," said Milt, "don't stand here. Go fetch the horses." He slowly grinned. "I'll wait . . . got some name-callin' to do, an' it always embarrasses me to have folks listen in. Go on."

Buck went. He got back to their animals, untied them, mounted his, and led Milt's horse back to the stunted paloverde. As he reined in close, he said: "Get it all out of your system?"

Milt reached, caught his reins, put his left hand around the saddle horn, and gingerly tested his wounded leg. During Buck's absence he'd fashioned a bandage out of his handkerchief and several strips of shirt tail. Pain made sweat pop out on his upper lip.

"No, I didn't get it all out of my system," he growled, using both arms to drag himself up over leather and grunting with the pain of it. "I never even got a good look at him. I came around that little paloverde, and the danged feller was lyin' flat under a sagebrush clump. I saw movement out of the corner of my eye and jumped . . . but too late. He drilled me and run out like a scairt rabbit." Milt grimaced as his injured leg dangled, and his mount moved a little, getting squarely under Milt's considerable weight.

"I'd give twenty dollars for another go-round with that damned. . ."

"Let's head out," Buck said, cutting across his pardner's garrulity. "We've got to get back to town and warn everyone."

Milt reined around. He sat gingerly with his injured leg disengaged. Each step of his horse was agony. After they'd gone on a mile, he said: "Buck, I can't make any kind of time. You lope on ahead and pass the word. I'll come along as best I can."

"Not a chance," responded his pardner. "You'll be pokin' along a couple of hours from now and those Comancheros will come across you. After that, you'll wish you only had a punctured leg. They know more slow ways for a man to die than the Indians know."

"Well, then," muttered Milt, fishing in a pocket and dredging up his tobacco sack, "make me a cigarette. Next to a slug of Taos Lightning, I need a smoke the worst."

Buck, who rarely smoked, looped his reins and went to work. The cigarette he fashioned and handed across took Milt's thoughts from his pain for a moment, long enough for him critically to examine this lumpy, misshapen object before popping it into his mouth, and say: "Hell, if you don't shoot any better'n you manufacture smokes . . . we're all doomed."

They exchanged a smile over this, Milt lit up, and Buck said: "We've got to lope for a couple of miles or we'll never get off this desert in time. You up to it, Milt?"

"No, but I'll do it."

They rocketed along, silent except for Milt's occasional anguished profanity, had covered easily two miles when, somewhere far back, they heard that pistol signal again—two quick shots, an interval of silence, then two more shots.

Buck slowed, slewed around in his saddle, and looked back.

"Now what?" muttered Milt. "What was that for?"

"They sent a scout on ahead," explained Buck. "He's found the place where you were. Evidently the feller who shot you thought he'd done a better job than he actually did." Buck straightened back forward. "You can thank your lucky stars, Milt. If you were still back there an' they found you . . ."

"Yeah," growled Milt. "Yeah, I understand. They'd kill me an inch at a time. Say, hadn't we better try loping for another couple of miles, Buck?" At Buck's quick look, big Milt shrugged his shoulders. "All of a sudden this leg's feeling better an' better."

They hastened north, pushing their animals hard. Somewhere in the night, far back, was a band of murderers in eager pursuit of two horsemen who had chased, and nearly caught, Cleve Brownell's messenger. These were the Comancheros, grisliest killers known to the Southwest.

SIXTEEN

They came out of the sooty night near Tenawa to see many lights. Closer on toward town they sighted considerable activity. Buck, gazing steadily ahead, wished it were possible for them to split up, for one of them to go in search of Wyatt Kilgore out at the Fishhook, while the other remained in Tenawa to pass word of an imminent visitation from Brownell's Comanchero allies. But Milt was not up to this, so they passed into Tenawa from the south, were angling off toward an alleyway that ran behind town, and encountered Kilgore.

"Hey," said Milt in mild surprise. "Look yonder."

Buck and Kilgore sighted each other at the same time, both hearkening to Milt's words. Kilgore was sitting a saddle horse in the shadowy roadway with one of his cowboys. He stepped down, paced swiftly to Buck's side, and asked the obvious question. He seemed a little breathless.

Buck shook his head. "Got away, Wyatt. He drilled Milt in the leg and got away."

"Then the Comancheros'll be coming."

"They're about two miles behind us," agreed Buck. He looked northward up the road. "What's going on here?" he asked.

Tenawa's main roadway was brightly lighted. Even the mercantile establishments, which normally closed their doors with the arrival of early evening, were open for business. People came and went, mostly men and mostly armed with carbines and rifles.

"I been busy," said Kilgore, twisting also to gaze over the town. "I got my boys an' rode in here. The cowmen were ridin' in from every direction when we got here." Kilgore paused, spat aside, then made a little grim nod with his head. "That's all it took, Buckley. The townsmen were ready, but they wouldn't do anything by themselves. Now folks are united. They want Brownell killed or run out."

"Where is he?" Milt asked, easing down out of the saddle. "I'd kind of like to knock him down an' run up an' down his belly myself."

Kilgore shook his head. "Gone," he growled. "When I got here, he was gone. He'd come back to town from the Baylor place, but he didn't stay long, folks say." Kilgore tilted his head. "I got two of his spies in the constable's office, though, locked up. One is Sam Potter, the feller he had out at my place, the other is a bartender he'd planted in Charley Gifford's Lone Star Saloon."

Buck sat there, watching Tenawa's activity, running several things through his mind. "He'd head for the Comanchero camp, Wyatt. By now he's probably met 'em on their way to Tenawa."

"Well," Kilgore rationalized grimly, "if they got to

come, I'll be glad if he's with 'em. There's quite a herd of us as would like one more crack at him."

A stooped, shuffling figure carrying a long-barreled rifle passed out of nearby gloom, crossed a lighted path of roadway, and faded into gloom again. Milt and Buck saw this man. Kilgore saw him, too, and said softly: "Even Frank Hardesty wants to see Brownell once more."

Buck watched that slumped figure pass along and pain stirred in him. He'd known Frank Hardesty in other years. Frank had been a strong, good-humored man with much to be thankful for.

"I hope he does," murmured Buck. "I hope Frank sees him first."

Three riders moving abreast down the roadway with carbines across their laps swerved over at sight of Kilgore. They were range riders and one of them, a genial-looking, very ugly man, squinted over at Buck.

"I knew you were back," this man said triumphantly. "I saw you ride across in front of me night before last, Buckley. I even said it was you, but the fellers I was with said it couldn't be . . . that you'd died up at Dodge City."

Buck nodded. "Hello, Joe," he said dryly. "Well, I'll tell you, I did die up at Dodge, but that Kansas ground is so darned stony, I just got out of the grave, saddled up, and lit out for home."

The cowboy called Joe made a broad smile. One of his companions laughed and the other one, not the laughing type, brushed this exchange aside to say: "We got a little trouble going for us around here. Maybe you've heard."

Kilgore snorted at this and Milt looked wry. But Buck said impassively: "Yeah, I've heard. Where are you fellers riding to?"

"Thought we'd drift a little ways south of town an' see if we can see or hear anything."

"Y'all don't drift too far. There's a big band of Comancheros out there, headin' for Tenawa."

Those three cowboys sobered instantly. One of them said: "Are you plumb sure?"

This nettled vinegary Wyatt Kilgore. He swore, then said: "Of course, he's sure. He's seen 'em, an' his pardner here's got a leaded leg from one of 'em. Now you boys don't go more than a thousand yards below town, stay together, an', when you hear 'em comin', you dust it back here and raise the yell."

Kilgore turned as an aproned, fat, and heavily perspiring storekeeper came up. "What is it?" he asked testily.

"I'm sold out of ammunition, Wyatt, an' those freighters are back with all the women and kids they could round up from the outlyin' ranches."

"Well," demanded Kilgore, "what do you want me to do about it? Go on back to your store, make dang' certain the womenfolk and the kids are tucked out of harm's way, then take off that silly white apron unless you want your paunch riddled, take up your rifle, and join the others at keepin' watch."

The three riders drifted off southward, the merchant also departed, and Wyatt Kilgore looked around at Milt. "You come with me," he said. "Doc Barnes will likely be busy, but we'd better get that leg taken care of now."

Buck dismounted, took Milt's reins, and nodded at his pardner. "I'll be around when you're through," he said, and started along the roadway, leading their horses.

At the livery barn he encountered a tough band of bearded freighters. These were the men who had kept supply lines open into towns like Tenawa during the worst of the Comanche troubles. They were also the scarred veterans of many a brush with Mexican marauders and brigand bands of Comancheros. He did not know these men, but he heard them talking and learned that these were the men who had gone out with their wagons to fetch ranch families into town.

Later, walking through this town which he had not set foot into since early the previous spring, he encountered men who recognized him, who halted to stare, and sometimes to speak. He also ran across a number of cowboys he'd known on the trail. He did not have much to say and neither did the others. There would, perhaps, be plenty of time to rub elbows at the bars later on. Right now, everyone was imbued with a spirit of exultation, as though after a long time they were eagerly up in arms against oppression.

This was the nature of Texans. They had demonstrated it before under similar and other, different circumstances. Once convinced of the need for united action, once united in their fighting resolve, they would spend their strength and their blood to triumph and thus far in their turbulent history no one had ever prevailed against them, numbers notwithstanding, once they took up their guns.

There was almost a carnival atmosphere to

Tenawa's warm, faintly moonlighted night. Men who would be fighting savagely within an hour stood here and there in little groups, talking softly and smiling at one another. If there was fear, it was not visible among the tough range men who were in the majority upon the plank walks.

"Buckley Baylor!"

A heavily built older man with one of those old-time, fiercely upswept Longhorn mustaches stepped forth, planted his legs wide to block Buck's advance, and showed even white teeth in a wide grin. This was Charles Gifford, owner of Tenawa's most popular saloon, the Lone Star.

Buckley gripped Gifford's big hand and dropped it. "Hello, Charley," he said, thinking back to what his mother had told him about Gifford's trying to help rehabilitate Carol Hardesty after Brownell tired of her.

"Good to see you, boy. It seems, sometimes, like you rode off ten years ago. We heard you got killed."

Buck nodded, looking steadily and unsmilingly at the barman. "It has been a long time, Charley. How does a feller measure time? By months, or by events?"

Gifford's smile wilted and died out. He understood about the turning knife blade that was bringing on Buck's resurrected anguish at the sight of him. "Something I also learned, when I was growin' up," he said quietly. "I was a little like you in those days. I didn't have a whole lot to hang onto, Buck . . . and it got taken away from me about like it did from you. Only in those days it was the damned Injuns did it, not white men. I learnt that life singles some folks out and piles grief on top of grief for them, while other folks go blithely through life without much pain ever seekin' 'em out." Charley Gifford lifted thick shoulders and let them drop. He looked Buckley squarely in the eye. "You got to live to be near fifty before you get the reasons sorted out, son."

"What are the reasons, Charley?"

"A real man never becomes one until he's been through the hardening and tempering process, Buck. This land's never had a leader worth his salt who hasn't come through a mile of tears and heartbreaks."

"That doesn't fit us, Charley. We're not leaders. We're just plain men who want to live and let live."

Gifford gently shook his head at this. "A leader doesn't have to live in the White House or lead a brigade of cavalry on a white horse, Buckley. He can be the feller who runs a saloon and plots against the Brownells of this world. Or he can be the young buck who comes back to find his pa murdered and . . . and other things gone sour for him, too, things that make him spark resistance and start the fight for all of us." Gifford ran a big hand absently under his fierce, old-fashioned mustache. "Wyatt and I talked a while this evening, Buck. We discussed you, among other things." Gifford straightened up, dropped his hand to the hip-holstered gun he wore, and, although his face did not smile, his voice brightened a little as he said: "Go on over to the variety store. Your ma and Frazier's girl are over there. I saw 'em come in with the freighters. They'll want to know how it is with you."

Gifford raised a big paw, tapped Buck lightly on the shoulder, and moved off northward, his gait rolling, his thick silhouette blocking out light, his usually gregarious expression pensive and thoughtful and a little sad. He was thinking with some bitterness that youth in this raw frontier world required boys to become men before they'd scarcely learned what youth was.

Wyatt Kilgore and big Milt Bond stepped out of Dr. Carter Barnes's little building and saw Buck heading out across the roadway toward the yonder variety store. Wyatt held out a hand.

"Don't call," he said. "His ma's over there. Her and Justin Frazier's girl."

Milt, with a big breath stored up, slowly exhaled. His leg had been cleanly cared for and efficiently bandaged. It protested his every step, but he no longer considered it an impediment to whatever he had to do this night. He fished around for his tobacco sack, twisted up a smoke, offered the sack to Wyatt, got a negative head shake, and returned it to his pocket.

Around them the village was beginning to settle into a waiting mood. Most of that earlier activity had atrophied. Men stood calmly now, some in orange lamplight along the roadway, some in dripping darkness.

There were no women or children on the walkways at all. Even tethered horses had been taken away and put where errant bullets would not find them. Some of the stores were dark. Men stood in those gloomy recessed doorways with pale star shine glinting wetly off weapons. Occasionally a rider or a group of riders would appear belatedly, coming in off the roundabout plain, but after a while these men stopped arriving in Tenawa.

Wyatt Kilgore balanced there upon the plank walk's edge, looking north, looking south, taking the pulse of the night, keening the spirit of the town. Milt stolidly smoked at his side.

"How much longer, you reckon?" Kilgore asked, his usual testy tone altered to a softer, duller timbre.

"Not much longer," Milt answered. "Maybe fifteen minutes." He blew out a bluish cloud, ran his gaze over the town, and said: "Looks pretty normal for a cow town this time o' night. Not too many lights, not too much excitement."

Kilgore shifted his stance. "Brownell'll send a scout ahead. Maybe it'll look like that to him."

"I hope so. If it does, they'll come bustin' right up the main roadway off the desert to the south and find themselves smack dab in the middle of the damnedest ambush I ever saw, instead of hittin' an unsuspectin' and defenseless town."

Kilgore nodded, saying nothing for a while. "Strange thing about killin'," he eventually murmured. "When you got it in your heart, you're real eager. When it's this close and you can taste it in your mouth . . . it leaves you with a bitterness you'd just as soon not have at all."

"What's the alternative? Leavin' the Comancheros to run free and work their devilment some other place?"

"No. We'll do it, Milt. We'll do it because we got to, but that doesn't make it pleasant."

Milt finished the cigarette, dropped it, and ground it out under a boot heel. He drew in a big breath of good night air and gazed somberly across to where Buckley had disappeared into the variety store.

SEVENTEEN

Mahalia saw her son enter the store and moved to intercept him. Off to one side among other women Kathleen also saw Buck's lanky frame briefly darken the roadside doorway, then drift on into the little room with its buzz of low talk and its crowd of women and children. She let the talk eddy around her, watching mother and son come together in a gloomy corner. She allowed them a moment alone, then started forward.

There were two coal-oil lamps burning on counters in this place, neither one shedding a whole lot of light and too distant from one another to co-operate in brightening the gloomy store. Some of the younger children had been bedded down in corners and out-of-the-way places. Most of the women, seeking solace in talk, were clustered in tight little groups. There was a closeness here that seemed greater than the tension out where the men were. Buck noticed it as his mother stopped, put her strong face forward, and asked where he'd gone after the fight at the barn.

"After one of them," he said, looking over Mahalia's

head. "He got away, though, after shooting Milt in the
leg." Buck finally saw Kathleen, working toward them
through the others. "I reckon you found Justin," he said
to his mother.

Mahalia nodded, looking expressionless. "That was
your carbine in his lap, Son. Your pa gave you that gun
when you turned seventeen."

"Yes."

Mahalia's smoky-gray eyes flicked with solemn
understanding. "I'm glad you did it that way," she
said. "There's been enough bitterness. When this is
over with, there shouldn't be anything left behind to
fester."

"She didn't suspect anything?"

"Why should she? She didn't know about her father
and Brownell. She thinks he died a hero . . . died fighting against Brownell."

"Maybe we'd best talk about it later, Ma. She's coming over."

Mahalia had the last word: "There's nothing more to
talk about. It's over and done with. Justin died for the
right cause. That's the end of it."

Kathleen came up. There was no indication that she
had cried, but shadows lay deeply in her eyes and she
was very solemn. She didn't mention her father, either,
for which Buck was thankful. She said instead: "There
is a rumor of Comancheros, Buck."

"It's more than a rumor," he replied, looking fully
down at her. "Milt and I ran across 'em to the south.
It's a good-sized band."

Kathleen nodded, accepting this, turning a little to
look at the others, then swinging her attention back.

"You be careful," she said, and laid a hand upon Mahalia's arm.

"And you, too," he said gently. "Kathy, I'm sorry about your pa."

"That was the way he would have wanted it, Buck."

"Yes."

Mahalia broke in to ask about Milt's injury. Buck was relieved at this topical switch and explained that Milt would be uncomfortable for a few weeks but otherwise he'd be all right. He took off his hat, held it in both hands, and looked at Kathleen. She seemed very desirable now, standing in soft shadows, looking calm and mature and somehow much older. He couldn't even make out those little girlhood freckles.

Mahalia looked at her son, at Kathleen, turned and walked away. Somewhere outside a man's quick, high cry rang down the roadway. Buck heard but made no move.

"We never got to take that ride," he said.

"No, but then it's only been a couple of days. We'll take it one of these days, Buckley."

"Yeah."

"Remember that arroyo where we found the Indian cave?"

"Yes."

"Well, I ride there every once in a while. It reminds me of the times when we were kids and used to play over there."

Buck looked at his hat. "Kathleen, now that your pa's gone and all. . ."

"Yes?"

195

"I'd be glad to help you round up . . . stuff like that, if you'd want me to."

"I'd want you to, Buck."

Again that high cry of alarm rang down the yonder roadway. This time running, booted feet striking harshly upon the outside plank walk brought Buck back to peril and danger. He put on his hat, felt for something to say which would give her some idea of what lay in his heart, failed dismally, and turned away with a brusque little nod, bound for the outside roadway.

Mahalia came up and solidly took her place beside old Justin Frazier's girl. "You'll never get used to the way they look at you, all tongue-tied-like, then walk away. All the while they're gone, you'll be putting words into their mouths and praying with your whole heart they'll come back to you alive." She took Kathleen's arm and led her back from the store front. "They're heartache from the day you first see them until the day . . . you bury them . . . but you wouldn't have it any other way."

"Mahalia, I love him."

"I know, honey, I know."

"Since we were very young. . . ."

"I saw it, Kathy. I saw it and I suffered right along with you. They're so blind sometimes, so blind and so unthinking, but a good man's love is the finest thing on this earth." Mahalia paused, saw the forming scald of tears, and closed her work-roughened hands over Kathleen's arm. "You'll know these things someday and I'll be there to guide you as much as I dare. Now come along. We can't stand out here in the open."

Beyond the storefront three cowboys came racing

along from the desert south of town. They cried out as they sped northward, saying a big band of hard-riding armed men were in sight just beyond Tenawa. Wyatt Kilgore and Milt Bond saw and heard and moved off the plank walk, carbines in hand to pass over where Buck Baylor stood with Charley Gifford outside the variety store. When these four came together, they were brisk with one another.

"Go pass the word," Kilgore said sharply to Gifford. "Tell the men to stay down, to hold their fire until every last one of Brownell's murderers is in the roadway." Charley whipped around and hastened away.

Wyatt hefted his weapon, scowled, and looked up and down the roadway where townsmen and cattlemen were getting into their positions. Milt, finishing a similar inspection, said to Buck: "This time . . . Brownell . . . none of those others until we got him. All right?"

Buck nodded. A slouched, old-looking man came up to them, peered around, and passed along as far as a doorway where several other men also waited. Frank Hardesty's long-barreled rifle stood nearly to his shoulder as he halted, looked at the others in that doorway, then stepped away, out to the very edge of the plank walk where a water trough stood, knelt there, and began examining the load in his musket.

Milt would have said something to Hardesty, but Buck stopped him. "Leave him be. Sure, he's exposed, but that's the way he wants it."

Kilgore put up his hand. "Listen," he said.

They heard that solid sound of many running horses coming forth out of the night toward the south. Milt cocked his head, lifted his carbine, looked behind for a place of concealment, and said to Wyatt: "Brownell's scout wasn't very observant. He's leading 'em right up the roadway."

"That's the way we wanted it, isn't it?"

Milt nodded. He said very softly: "Like shooting ducks on a mill pond, but if they're that stupid, then I'm mean enough to take advantage of it."

A man's savage scream, sounding like the panther it was meant to sound like, broke over that oncoming thunder of shod hoofs and a gunshot erupted as Brownell's merciless Comancheros swept into the south end of what they thought was another unsuspecting and defenseless village.

A little ripple of gunfire followed this typical Comanchero announcement that marauders were striking. Milt and Wyatt brushed against Buckley, moving toward the recessed variety store doorway. Buck turned, too, after sighting that road full of charging renegades. He had been looking particularly for a well-dressed man. He had seen him, too. As he swung away, he called toward the water trough: "Frank, he's in the lead. Don't miss!"

A flashing burst of gunfire broke out along both sides of the roadway. Those solidly packed raiders, confined between two opposing walkways, northbound and riding wildly lunging horses, returned this fire in a crimson volley.

North of Buck's doorway someone opened up prematurely with a shotgun. The throaty roar of this deadly weapon overrode all the other sounds now erupting in the soft-lighted night.

Glass tinkled and men cried out. Horses screamed in terror and in pain. Tenawa's opposite banks of storefronts did not allow this bedlam to dissipate in any direction but upward. It was terrifying and deafening. Brownell's Comancheros, nearly half a hundred strong, came at last to realize what they had ridden into. Behind them men on foot ran out into the roadway to seal off retreat. Ahead, near the northernmost limits of town, there stood a wagon barricade across the roadway with savagely blinking little red flashes.

"Trapped!" someone roared. "Fight clear!"

Behind his water trough Frank Hardesty let the crowding riders get up to him, even with him. He did not fire. Buck and Milt and Wyatt Kilgore saw raiders twist to throw lead toward Hardesty. They tried to beat these men to it, firing through a growing, acrid haze. Hardesty still did not open up. Water sprayed over him from the hurtling impact of bullets striking closely.

Then Hardesty, without hurry, with great deliberation, shouldered his rifle, snugged it back, and took long aim. Buck, nearly as fascinated by Hardesty's iron nerve as anything else around him, flung his gaze outward in the direction of that long barrel. He saw Brownell, sitting up there with his hat gone and his gun roaring, but only for the fleeting-most part of a second. Hardesty fired, staggered drunkenly from the impact, lowered his rifle slowly, and ignored the tumult to watch Cleve Brownell draw upright on his horse, swing his head in total astonishment, lock his gaze upon the man who had shot him, then drop from sight under the hoofs of the Comancheros' horses around him, surging and writhing and fighting to get clear.

Milt was yelling something but Buck could not make it out, nor did he try very hard for now the full press of that mingled mass of panicked horses and desperately clawing gunmen was even with him. He shot his handgun empty, grabbed a carbine, and levered it empty, too. This was sheer slaughter, but it was also very deadly for the town's defenders. Bullets struck with a ripping sound into wood siding. They shattered windows with a frightening crash, and they also hit men's bodies with a jarringly meaty sound.

Wyatt Kilgore stepped out, swung his leg, and kicked open the variety store doorway. The three of them tumbled inside, slammed the door, and dropped down near a broken window. Somewhere behind them a number of children were screaming in terror. Somewhere behind them, too, Mahalia Baylor's deep, calm voice was holding those crouched and terrified women motionless.

A large, brutish-looking man was unhorsed and rolled as far as the plank walk, there to spring up in a fighting crouch. Buck recognized this as one of the outlaws who had escaped from the earlier fight in front of his barn. He raised his pistol, but not quickly enough. Milt dropped the renegade in his tracks, eased down to reload, and Wyatt Kilgore fired himself empty, too. It was not a matter of aiming. Those writhing horsemen could not escape. It was simply a matter of pouring overpowering amounts of lead into that screaming, writhing tumult of men and animals.

A wild-eyed and hatless Mexican brigand with crossed bandoleers over his big chest jumped from his horse's back to the plank walk and made a desperate lunge for cover. Whoever had that shotgun north of the variety store let off both barrels. The Mexican wasn't shot down; he was literally blown in two.

Among the Comancheros came cries for quarter in two languages. Some of these scourges broke clear and threw themselves northward straight toward the wagon barricade, evidently preferring this hopeless gamble to the certainty of what was in store for them if taken alive. Not a one of those riders got within a hundred feet of the barricade; all died, along with their horses, in Tenawa's ghostly roadway.

That mass of humanity and horseflesh thinned out somewhat. Bodies of men and animals lay, not only in the roadway, but upon both plank walks. In fact, a dead horse lay where he'd sprung when the slug struck him, blocking the entrance to Gifford's Lone Star Saloon. His rider, unhurt but pinned by the leg and unable to move, caught four slugs before he could surrender, if that had been his intention. He jerked each time he was hit, and afterward lay face up, relaxed and peaceful.

Wyatt Kilgore pushed his arm out the window to fire at a dodging, running Comanchero, went over backward before he could squeeze the trigger, and got up onto his knees, looking astonished. There was a round dark hole and a quick trickle of crimson from his right shoulder.

EIGHTEEN

The cry of attacking Comancheros was gradually replaced by cowmen and storekeepers who emerged from their battlements to raise the Rebel yell of embattled Texans the world over. With nothing left to lose but their lives, a squad of unhorsed Comancheros made up a solid rank and retreated steadily northward up the littered roadway toward the wagon barricade, firing at every muzzle blast that blossomed toward them from storefronts, from doorways, even from rooftops. They were cut down one at a time; they died hard, each one of them firing as long as nerve lasted and muscles responded.

Inside the buildings men pushed to get out, to face these merciless marauders in the last vivid enactment of this bloody meeting. Even Wyatt Kilgore, shrugging off Milt's solicitation and Buck's restraining hand, went out of the variety store to take his stand in eerie moonlight and swap shots with the downed men in the roadway who, although too badly injured to escape, fought on until, one and two at a time, they were killed.

A clutch of Comancheros, who had made it into the

doorless front maw of the livery barn opposite Charley Gifford's saloon, were the last holdouts. They had shot out the lamps and were in total darkness.

Wyatt called Buck and Milt out to him. "Go around back," he ordered. "Don't let a one of 'em get out through the rear alley. I'll gather some men an' seal 'em off in front."

Buck led off in a trot. Milt, his leg bleeding again under its bandage, hobbled after him. Other men joined these two, guessing their purpose and destination.

From Gifford's saloon a number of dogged defenders kept the Comancheros in the barn occupied long enough, too long, in fact, for when Buck, Milt, and the men with them got around behind the barn, bullets were whipping straight down through the wide runway and slashing outward into the night beyond. It was, for a time, as dangerous for the men outside as for the Comancheros inside.

Wyatt Kilgore, though, got to the saloon and profanely ordered those townsmen and range men inside to hold their fire. With the cessation of this firing, Tenawa became utterly silent for a long moment. It was such a startling, abrupt, and unexpected stillness that in some ways it was louder in men's heads than the shooting had been.

Buck sidled up close to the livery barn's rear doorway, flattened there, and called for the Comancheros to throw out their guns and end it. While awaiting a reply, Buck heard men calling back and forth around front in the roadway. He heard boots striking upon the plank walks again and the impact of voices where men walked out among the dead and the dying.

"We're coming out!" cried a Comanchero from somewhere inside the livery barn. "Don't shoot. We're coming out."

"Guns first or you'll end up like your friends out in the roadway."

The guns came, a wide assortment of them but mostly six-guns and Winchester saddle carbines. Buck and the men standing out there with him considered these weapons. Milt said: "Not a belly gun among 'em an' you know better'n that."

Buck swung around toward the wide opening again. "All right, come out one at a time ... and any man with a hideout gun on him gets shot on the spot."

For a little while there was no sound from inside. A little nickel-plated under-and-over .41-caliber Derringer sailed out to land among the other surrendered weapons in the alleyway. Big Milt smiled wolfishly at this. Other concealed, short-barreled weapons were also thrown out. With them came an assortment of wicked-looking, thin-bladed Mexican knives.

"Regular damned arsenal," a townsman growled.

From inside, his voice sounding hollow, a Comanchero called: "We're plumb clean now! Ready for us to walk out o' here?"

"One at a time," Buck responded. "And remember ... one wrong move and you're dead. Now come out of there!"

They came, a filthy, ragged, sweaty group of twelve men, some swarthy from the suns of Mexico, some lighter, some in-between, but every one of them vicious-looking and deadly, every one of them a killer and worse.

Among the defenders, at sight of this savage crew, there arose a murmur for instant lynching. Milt blocked this by planting his big frame before their captives and looking menacingly around. He said nothing; big Milt Bond didn't have to say anything. He looked—and he was—the equal of any three townsmen in a raw fight. Clearly he was now ready to back up that disapproving scowl. The lynch talk died down to a whisper and even that eventually faded out.

They herded the prisoners around front. There, Wyatt Kilgore, his shirt red-sticky and his angry eyes glassy with fatigue, viewed the survivors of Brownell's bandit ring with an unrelenting toughness. Around him other defenders showed up.

"Lock 'em in the constable's office," Wyatt snarled to Buck and Milt. "Before I weaken an' donate the lariats for the lot of 'em."

Men came forth with lamps. They walked gingerly out into the roadway. They hunted up the injured and carried them away. Except for the desultory run of their talk, Tenawa was still breathlessly quiet.

Charley Gifford lent his considerable strength, along with four others, to dragging that Comanchero and his dead horse away from the Lone Star's entrance. Afterward, Charley strode inside, threw his spindle doors wide open, and stood, wide-legged, both big fists on his hips, and roared out in a bull-bass voice that for the remainder of this night all drinks were on him.

Men came trooping along still with carbines in their hands to take advantage of Charley's offer. Elsewhere, other men were surveying the damage to their town, to their stores and their inventories. Among the range men there was a certain amount of congregating apart from the townsmen to compare recollections and tales of near hits and near misses.

Buckley and Milt herded their captives to the jailhouse, locked them inside, and stood for a little while before the door, waiting for the milling men around them to take the hint, to drift up toward Charley's bar and join in downing free liquor. As the last of those men walked off, Milt put aside his carbine, worked up a cigarette, lit it, and with his head far back exhaled a great gust of pale smoke.

"What a night," he said softly. "What a damned night. You know, Buck, if someone ever told me something like this, and said they'd dreamed it, I wouldn't even believe it then."

Buck ran a soiled sleeve over his face, pushed back his hat, and held out his hand for Milt's tobacco sack. He stood loose and exhausted and let down, making his cigarette. Milt watched this with professional interest, shook his head as he held a match, and said: "You still can't roll cigarettes, but I take back what I hinted at earlier . . . that you might not be any better at shooting."

They stood in the formless night, watching Tenawa dig out, sweep its broad roadway clear of the battle's wreckage, and, too completely dragged out even to speak for a long time, let the quiet night form solidly around them. Wyatt Kilgore came along with a fresh bandage under his ragged shirt. For once he had nothing sharp to say. He, too, rolled a cigarette from Milt's makings, lit up, and held the smoke between thin lips with his eyes pinched nearly closed.

"We lost three dead and seven hurt."

Milt and Buck absorbed this fragment stolidly.

"They lost at least thirty dead." Wyatt removed the cigarette, critically examined its glowing tip, and added: "None wounded." He popped the smoke back into his mouth, brightened his tone, and said: "Buckley, your ma and Kathleen are waitin' over at the livery barn. They got Charley Gifford's top buggy borrowed for the ride home. They're waiting for you, boy. I said I'd hunt you up."

Milt gave a sudden start, winced, and rolled his eyes at Kilgore. The shorter, wispier man looked up with a quick, puzzled scowl. "What the hell's wrong with you?" he demanded.

"It's m'leg. It's bleedin' again, an' I can't ride out to the Baylor place on horseback."

"Well," said Kilgore, "that's no problem. Come along. I'll get you a buggy at the livery barn."

Buck turned and looked at Milt, his expression one of deep concern. He offered Milt a hand but the big man shook his head. "You go on ahead. I'll lean on Wyatt."

Buck led off, walking northward from the constable's office. Behind him big Milt nearly dwarfed vinegary Wyatt Kilgore as he limped along, leaning downward. These two had progressed less than a hundred feet when Wyatt gasped under that solid weight.

"Dang it, it can't hurt *this* much, Milt. Quit leanin' so much. That's my wounded shoulder, you blamed ox."

Milt straightened up at once, squinted far ahead where Buckley was turning in, and, stepping out swiftly, said: "Come on, Wyatt. Dang it all, hurry up, will you?"

Kilgore whipped along nearly trotting. He suddenly looked down, looked up, and swore with feeling. "That leg don't hurt you one damned bit," he snapped. "What're you tryin' to . . . ?"

"Not so loud," broke in Milt, who slowed and bent to put his lips close to Kilgore's head. "I'll need Miz Baylor to ride with me in the buggy, you see, otherwise I might up and plumb pass out from loss of blood." He straightened back, beamed down at Wyatt, waiting for Kilgore to comprehend.

But Wyatt's wits were too dulled for this byplay. He said waspishly: "You danged Yankee boys are too devious for us honest an' forthright Texans. Now just what the devil are you up to?"

Milt rolled his eyes heavenward. "Dense, that's what you Texans are, like a block of wood between the ears. Listen, Buck and Kathleen ought to ride back together . . . now do you understand?"

Kilgore's face cleared gradually. By the time they were nearing the livery barn entrance where two rigs were waiting, Wyatt's dark eyes were bright with approval. He darted ahead where Mahalia was standing beside one of the rigs and swept off his hat to her. Behind him, big Milt made his painful way forward much slower, grimacing with the sheer agony this walking was causing him.

The other buggy suddenly started forward. Buck leaned out and waved. Beside him, Kathleen sat with her head tilted back upon the seat, noticing only the congealed stars overhead in the purple heavens.

Mahalia looked at Wyatt Kilgore, standing there with his mouth open, his gaze following that other buggy, then switched her grave attention to Milt as Buck's limping pardner came up and leaned heavily upon a wheel. She said, after a careful assessment of those two grimy faces: "Too bad your relapse came on so quickly, Milton. I saw you a dozen times tonight moving without any trouble at all. Well, get up into the rig. I'll drive you home and fix a good hot mustard poultice to draw the inflammation away."

Milt straightened up, looking incredulous. "Mustard poultice?" he croaked. "Ma'am, believe me, there's not a blessed thing wrong with this leg."

Mahalia let Wyatt hand her up into the buggy. She eased down, arranged her skirt, and took up the lines. "I know that," she said, without looking around where Milt was climbing up beside her, her voice flat and matter-of-fact. "But maybe the poultice will teach you not to try and hoodwink someone."

"Hoodwink . . . who?"

"Me, young man, me. Did you think for one minute I was going to ride with those two and spoil their one good moment of this terrible night? Of course, I wasn't. But I didn't go about it like you and Wyatt did. I'd already made arrangements for this rig."

Mahalia gave Kilgore a curt nod, flicked the lines, and drove off, her face set as always but her eyes soft and gentle, and just a little damp.

About the Author

Lauran Paine who, under his own name and various pseudonyms has written over nine hundred books, was born in Duluth, Minnesota, a descendant of the Revolutionary War patriot and author, Thomas Paine. His family moved to California when he was young and his apprenticeship as a Western writer came about through the years he spent in the livestock trade, rodeos, and even motion pictures, where he served as an extra because of his expert horsemanship in several films starring movie cowboy Johnny Mack Brown. In the late 1930s, Paine trapped wild horses in northern Arizona and even, for a time, worked as a professional farrier. Paine came to know the Old West through the eyes of many who had been born in the previous century, and he learned that Western life had been very different from the way it was portrayed on the screen. "I knew men who had killed other men," he later recalled. "But they were the exceptions. Prior to and during the Depression, people were just too busy eking out an existence to indulge in Saturday-night brawls." He served in the U.S. Navy in the Second World War and began writing for Western pulp magazines following his discharge. It is interesting to note that all of his earliest novels (written under his own name and the pseudonym Mark Carrel) were published in the British market and he soon had as strong a following in that country as in the United States. Paine's Western fiction is characterized by strong plots, authenticity, an apparently effortless ability to construct situation and character, and a preference for building his stories upon a solid foundation of historical fact. *Adobe Empire* (1956), one of his best novels, is a fictionalized account of the last twenty years in the life of trader William Bent and, in an off-trail way, has a melancholy, bittersweet texture that is not easily forgotten. In later novels like *The White Bird* and *Cache Cañon*, he has shown that the special magic and power of his stories and characters have only matured along with his basic themes of changing times, changing attitudes, learning from experience, respecting nature, and the yearning for a simpler, more moderate way of life.

LAURAN PAINE

GATHERING STORM

The two novels collected in this exciting volume capture perfectly the power and magic of Lauran Paine's work. His characters come alive, his plots create suspense, and his descriptions of the Old West are second to none. The title character in *The Calexico Kid* is a bandit who remains a mystery. Even those who have seen him cannot agree on what he looks like. How, then, can anyone bring him to justice? In *Gathering Storm*, two gunfighters arrive in a quiet range town within minutes of each other. One gunfighter in town is bad enough, but two can only mean trouble. Deadly trouble.

Dorchester Publishing Co., Inc.
P.O. Box 6640
Wayne, PA 19087-8640

_____5341-1
$4.99 US/$6.99 CAN

Please add $2.50 for shipping and handling for the first book and $.75 for each additional book. NY and PA residents, add appropriate sales tax. No cash, stamps, or CODs. Canadian orders require $2.00 for shipping and handling and must be paid in U.S. dollars. Prices and availability subject to change. **Payment must accompany all orders.**

Name: _____

Address: _____

City: _____ State: _____ Zip: _____

E-mail: _____

I have enclosed $_____ in payment for the checked book(s).

   For more information on these books, check out our website at www.dorchesterpub.com.
         _____ *Please send me a free catalog.*

GUNS IN
THE DESERT
LAURAN PAINE

This volume collects two exciting Lauran Paine Westerns in one book! In *The Silent Outcast*, Caleb Doorn is scouting for the U.S. Army when a small wagon train passes on its way to California. The train's path will take its members through Blackfoot country and the wagon master has foolishly taken a Blackfoot girl hostage. . . . In the title tale, Johnny Wilton, the youngest member of the Wilton gang, is shot and killed while attempting to set fire to the town. The surviving members of the gang plan a simple revenge—attack the town and kill everyone in it!

COTTON SMITH

DEATH RIDES A RED HORSE

What started as a simple trip for supplies has turned into a race against time and a fight to survive. Cole Kerry almost single-handedly broke up a raid on the town by a gang of outlaws. But one of them grabbed Cole's wife as they rode off, and Cole himself was shot in the back when he tried to track them down. Now it's up to his older brother, Ethan, to find Cole and rescue his wife—if they're still alive. It's a tough enough job for any man. Ethan isn't about to let the fact that he's blind stand between him and what he needs to do.